# The Rout of the Ollafubs

# The Rout of the Ollafubs

by
K. G. LETHBRIDGE

illustrated by
PAULINE BAYNES

FABER FANFARES

First published in 1964
by Faber and Faber Limited
3 Queen Square London WC1
First published in Fanfares edition 1978
Printed in Great Britain by
Jarrold & Sons Ltd, Norwich

© *K. G. Lethbridge*
1964

British Library Cataloguing in Publication Data

Lethbridge, Katherine Greville
The rout of the Ollafubs. – (Faber fanfares).
I. Title
823'.9'1J      PZ7.L/
ISBN 0–571–11273–0

To
Katharine, Nicolas and Emma

# Contents

# The Rout of the Ollafubs

Once upon a time there were two children called Skyboy and Littleflame, and they lived in a far-off country full of mountains and forests and rivers and strange animals and people. Their home was in a village, and usually they were busy looking after the sheep and goats, and to help them they had a big dog called Thunder. At the time of this story, Thunder was beginning to grow old, nobody knew quite how old, but soon after the children were born he had arrived on the doorstep of their home and he had looked after them when they were babies and he had looked after them ever since. He was the wisest, gentlest dog that ever lived, and he knew so much that everybody felt sure that he must have something to do with the fairies, but if he did he kept it to himself and never spoke about it.

It was late summer and the time for wild raspberries, and Skyboy and Littleflame had made themselves leaf-baskets and had gone to gather fruit far down the hill below the village. They had gone to a place which was called the Booming Rocks because on days when the wind blew, strange booming noises came from there which could be heard for miles around. Most people were afraid of the place and when the rocks were booming, would close their doors and huddle by the fire and tell each other stories of monstrous beings who used to live among the rocks in the days when their grandfathers and their great-grandfathers were alive. And at some time or another there certainly had been houses there, because there were ruins among the rocks and a crazily muddled kind of a place it must have been, with over- and under-ground passages all on different levels and tunnels and blocked doorways and gaping holes and crumbling walls, all making a kind of labyrinth half-hidden by nettles and thorns, easy to enter, but very hard to find a way out from. The raspberries grew among the thorns and nettles, and they grew in great clusters and bunches like no other raspberries, and it was these that tempted the children and made them forget their fears.

Thunder had been left up on the hillside where he could lie and watch the flocks and see the world spread out like a map in front of him. And as well as watching the flocks, he kept one eye on the children, although they were far away below him and most people would not have been able to see or hear them at all. But Thunder could see and hear a great deal more than you would have guessed through his long floppy ears and the bushy hair which hung over his eyes. He could hear things like birds laying their eggs into their nests and bees tucking pollen into their leg sacks, and he could see things like snipe hiding in the marsh grasses and green eels waving in the green river weed. And today he could hear the children's voices coming up from far below as they called to each other and he could see the tops of the bushes shaking when they caught hold of the branches to balance themselves. And as long as he could see and hear these things he was content. But suddenly the noises stopped, there were no more voices, no more movements among the branches, a cloud came over the sun and a restless wind blew over the hills and from far below came a muffled booming, very ominous and strange. Thunder lifted his head and listened and a feeling of great trouble and foreboding came over him.

The leaf baskets were almost full of raspberries and the children decided that they had picked enough. They started to climb back over the tumble-down walls, dawdling to gather tempting clusters of fruit and finding it hard to drag themselves away. One loaded bush they could not resist. It hung over the side of a ruined shaft and to reach the raspberries Littleflame stretched one arm as far as she could while with the other she clung to Skyboy to keep herself from falling. She clutched the fruit and as she clutched she felt the air coming up the shaft on her bare arm and it was hot.

'Feel this,' she said, and Skyboy leaned over the shaft and the draught was hot enough to lift the hair on his forehead.

'There must be something happening down below to make all that heat,' he said. 'Let's explore a bit and see if we can find anything.'

They hid their baskets of fruit under a wall and scrambled about among the ruins, and it was not long before they found two more hot shafts, and from one of these sparks were rising and the bushes around the top were scorched and shrivelled.

'It must be somebody's chimney,' said Littleflame. 'I wonder whoever can live here?'

'If we go on much farther, we shall forget where we left the raspberries,' said Skyboy. 'There's something queer about this place, I don't like it. Let's get away.'

But try as they would, they could not find their baskets

again. They climbed over and through the old walls and doorways; they went left, then right, then circled in their tracks, all the time getting more and more mixed in their directions and quite unable to get back to where they had started. All at once they came upon a kind of entrance which looked dark and forbidding and ran steeply downwards into the bowels of the labyrinth. A very strong smell of cooking came out of the entrance and at each side were mountainous middens, all the waste of some gigantic kitchen piled in disorder, bones and skins, decaying refuse and smashed utensils, and on the midden sat a group of lugubrious vultures tearing and pulling at the unpleasant remains. A cloud of satiated flies buzzed up into the air in front of the children, and the only cover between them and the entrance was a low broken wall and a few sparse brambles. Spellbound by what they saw, they crouched under the wall, and as they crouched they heard something coming up from down below, puffing and blowing its way to the top, cursing and grumbling as it came.

It was too late to escape, and in any case they were petrified with fear; the terrible being had already reached the opening and they could see its snout and long mulish ears as it scrambled up the last bit of the incline. Then it was right out in the open in front of them, huge and sleek with a long scaly tail and hoofs with claws, and it was slapping angrily at the flies as they settled on its face. The vultures hopped off heavily, took wing and soared away across the valley, and the dreadful creature flopped down with its back against a rubbish heap and started to fan itself with a monstrous spoon. Skyboy and Littleflame lay like cowering partridges, hardly daring to look but hearing the flop of the creature's hoofs and the swish of its tail as it hit out at the flies. It seemed to be dreadfully hot and out of temper and luckily too lazy to move from its seat. Soon the fresh air began to soothe it, and it laid its head back against the rubbish and went into a doze, snoring heavily with its mouth open showing its yellow teeth and dark blue tongue. When the snoring became regular Skyboy lifted his head and signed to Littleflame and they started to crawl away inch by inch under the wall, but they had hardly gone a yard before a deep vibrating booming filled the air which shuddered right down through their bones, not so much like a sound as like a strange element which was suffocating and enclosing them. The creature leaped straight from sleep into wild activity and was off down the hole like a stone from a sling. Holding their hands over their ears and hardly looking where they were going, Skyboy and Littleflame jumped up and started to run, or rather to tumble anywhere, anyhow, as long as they got away from that dreadful hole. It seemed easiest and quickest to go downwards and they were slithering backwards between rocks and thorns down a small gully when Skyboy felt two tremendous arms close round him like a vice, and a gruff and growly voice said indignantly:

'For Ole Spike's sake, do 'ee mind how thee be goin'! A roarin' an' a rushin' like a pair o' simps! Do'ee be deaf or daft?'

All of them went down in a shower of stones and landed up at the bottom of the gully rubbing their sore backs and looking startled. The children, who had thought that their last moment had come, looked up with enormous relief to see that the speaker was not an awful blue-tongued monster like the one they had seen on the kitchen middens, but a very large and very shaggy bear. After a long and awkward silence in which they all looked at each other very hard, the bear got up and shook himself, turned the children over with his paw, examined them and then set them upright again.

13

' 'Tisn't never no place for the likes o' you,' he said decidedly, 'wi' them Ollafubs a-bangin' their pots, an' a-bawlin' an' a-bellowin' for their grub. Do'ee come along o' I or 'tis you as'll be comin' along o' what's a darnside wusser!'

'There's something awful up there!' gasped Skyboy, pointing up the gully. 'We were trying to get away.'

'An' powerful awful it do be!' answered the bear. 'How come you do be nosin' around when you did oughter be tuck up tidy in your beds an' lyin' safe inside your little houses?'

'We only want to get back home,' said Littleflame in a very small voice. 'We're rather lost and could you please show us the way?'

'Gin you do go a-searchin' an' a-lookin' in this here place you'll be ate up sure as winkie. Them Ollafubs is always hungry. Do'ee come along o' I. 'Tis them as dursn't touch I.' The bear said this with a good deal of pride and certainly he looked a formidable mouthful.

Skyboy was about to protest, but it was obvious that the bear was a no-nonsense bear and would not stand for argument. He tucked one child firmly under each arm and started off at a rolling steady trot, down into the bed of a ravine which ran beside and below the Booming Rocks and the dwelling place of the Ollafubs.

The ravine grew very narrow and the cliff walls closed in on either side of them until there was only a thin strip of sky, and in places even this was hidden where rocks had fallen from above and become jammed between the faces, so that sometimes they were travelling in a tunnel. Presently the bear paused and set them down. He had been growling and grumbling a bit to himself and now he said:

' 'Tis like you do be middlin' dafty. I did oughter show 'ee what like them Ollafubs be.'

He lifted the children up and set them on his broad shoulders and told them to look. They found that light was coming out of a crack in the cliff wall which was partly hidden by bushes, and they pushed the twigs aside and peered in. An awesome sight was before them and although they could not see everything through so narrow a hole, they could see enough. They were looking into a great hall and on the far side was a line of fires and on the fires were steaming cauldrons. Ollafubs with spoons were walking up and down the line of cauldrons stirring the contents and fishing out great lumps of meat. Other Ollafubs—dozens and dozens of them—were sitting round the walls chewing and chewing and the sound of cracking bones was quite distinct. Littleflame shuddered and slipped down off the bear's shoulder. She had seen quite enough and so had Skyboy.

'An' don't 'ee never forget it!' said the bear sternly. He picked them up again and went on down the ravine to where it opened out between two towering pillars of rock on to a stony tussocky plain at the far side of which was a long dark line of forest. It was in this forest that the bear lived with his family and it was towards it that he was heading.

Neither Skyboy nor Littleflame remembered the last part of the journey. In fact, they knew nothing until they woke next day and found themselves cosily bedded in moss inside a cave with the sun filtering in through a doorway half hidden by trees. Littleflame lay for some time wondering wherever she was, slowly taking in the new sights and sounds. There was more on the patch of sunlight by the door than just the shadows of leaves. A small stout shadow with two prick ears lay across the floor and two paws were moving rhythmically to the sound of a husky voice. What was being chanted was not very distinct but in Littleflame's sleepy mind it sounded like:

'Ticky Tacky,
For an' Backy,
Gerrr Terrr,
Horrr an' Acky!'

Then she heard: 'I done drop her!' then an exclamation of
scorn—'Turnip!' then the chanting was resumed in another
rhythm while the shadow flailed its paws.

'Tosser Prosser
In the wasser
Man the pump
Up he jump.
Stuff him in
To the chin,
Back agin
An' I win!'

There was a happy shout of 'Apples an' Pears!' and the
shadow leaped over the floor, then settled down again, and
the chanting went on:

'Dopie Opie Cockadoodle
Got a rhyme inside her noodle;
Can't remember what it means;
Spits it out an' spills the beans!'

Littleflame was very curious. She sat up and crept towards
the doorway as quietly as she could and peeped out. There
on a flattened patch of ground outside sat four bear cubs in
a ring. They were playing a game of catch and throw with a
small polished knot of wood and as they played they chanted
their nonsensical little rhymes, keeping in time to the chanting. Suddenly the cub opposite caught sight of her,
dropped the knot of wood and bolted. Two others followed
and disappeared into a bush. The fourth cub stood his
ground gulping nervously. Skyboy joined Littleflame and

they sat smiling at the cub, trying to look as friendly as they could, while the cub stared back at them with round, frightened eyes. After a while, when he found they did not move, he said in a husky whisper:

'I be Cob. 'Tis them as do be powerful scarey.'

'Don't be scarey, Cob,' said Littleflame. 'We're not going to hurt anybody.'

'Why for do 'ee be come?' asked Cob after a pause.

'We didn't mean to come at all. A big bear just brought us.'

''Tis like 'twere our Ole Pad,' said Cob after another pause for consideration. 'He do bring us lots, conkers an' shells an' apricocks an' such.'

Neither Skyboy nor Littleflame felt like a conker, a shell or an apricot, but just then Mother Bear appeared carrying a honeycomb and the three other cubs crept from under the bush and followed her, peeping shyly from behind her quarters. She divided the comb into six great lumps which she squeezed up in her paws, pollen, honey, wax, grubs and all, and gave a lump to each cub and a lump to each child. They all sat eating and the honey that dripped to the ground was busily scooped up by the cubs and crammed into their mouths with earth, grass, leaves and anything else that happened to come with it. Mother Bear examined the children in front and behind while they were eating.

''Tisn't never you as done near be ate up!' she exclaimed, and clicking her tongue disapprovingly she shambled off.

'Who done near eat you up?' asked Cob.

'Awful things called Ollafubs,' answered Skyboy. 'They live in the Booming Rocks a long way off.'

The cubs chewed thoughtfully, looking at the children with respect.

''Tis them what our Mam done tell us of,' said another cub who had pale spectacle marks round his eyes which made him look very wise. His name was Tob. There was one girl cub called Nob and the fourth was a boy called Hob.

Well, here were Skyboy and Littleflame unexpectedly sitting among a family of bears, safe and sound, eating honeycomb and being treated as far as they could tell exactly like another pair of cubs. Littleflame was altogether delighted. She loved the cubs, she loved the novelty of honey and grubs for breakfast, the den was warm and cosy, she looked forward to a series of undisturbed and sunny days in which to chatter and play to her heart's content. A little niggling worry about what her mother would say might cloud her thoughts but did not stay with her for long. She got the cubs to teach her their rhymes and she joined them in their games, catching and throwing the wooden knobs which they called 'tossers' until she was almost as good at it as the cubs themselves.

The 'tossers' were greatly prized, were kept hidden under a tree root and taken out every day to be polished and admired. Littleflame, like all the other girls in her village, carried with her a small wooden spindle on which she spun the tufts of sheep's wool caught up in thorns into strong woollen yarn for weaving cloth. Now she tried to teach the cubs to spin and Nob, being a girl, persisted, and soon became quite good at it, so that Skyboy carved her out a spindle of her own of which she was very proud and which she always carried. Cob, Tob and Hob all tried spinning too, but they had not much patience and used the spindle as a 'tosser' and got themselves hopelessly wound up in a cat's cradle of wool. Just as Littleflame carried her spindle, so Skyboy carried his pipe on which he could play merry lilting tunes which made everybody want to dance, or sad far-off tunes which made them quiet and dreamy. The cubs were entranced by his playing and would sit motionless, listening for hours, and when he put his pipe down would creep up to him and plead: 'Play us a teeny bit more, do 'ee now!'

But Skyboy had much more than a little niggling worry inside his head. He was really anxious because his mother and father must think that they were lost, and if anybody searched and found those Ollafubs, whatever was going to happen? He tried to talk to Littleflame about his worries.

'Let's stay a few days,' she pleaded. 'They'll only think we've wandered off too far.'

'You stay and I'll go back by myself and send Thunder to bring you home.'

But she was not sure that she wanted to be left, delightful as life among the bears might be.

'Well, make up your mind,' said Skyboy. 'I'm going to tell Father Bear that I'm starting off to-morrow and thank him for taking care of us.'

But Father Bear was adamant. No charges of his were going off to risk being eaten up by Ollafubs and to make quite sure, he sat himself firmly at the entrance to the den and when he was tired of sitting, he told Mother Bear to sit instead.

'You kin bide if you've a mind,' said Tob anxiously, sensing the trouble. ''Tis us bears as'll fix 'ee wi' honey an' grub an' such.'

'We like it here very much,' answered Skyboy, feeling wretchedly ungrateful. 'But we can't stay for always. They'll think we're lost.'

''Tis you as isn't never lost,' said Tob gravely. ''Tis you as is found. You done be right here so's us kin see you.' There seemed no answer to this and more days passed, but on a sunny afternoon when the trees were turning gold and the gossamer cobwebs floating down in the still air, a chance of escape arrived unexpectedly. The cubs were playing in the den, Father Bear had gone off foraging, Mother

Bear, who was on guard duty, had her head firmly buried in an ant heap from which she was extracting the eggs. Skyboy took Littleflame's hand and looked at her and together they slipped off through the trees, and as soon as they were out of earshot they ran like the wind. They both felt sad and rather mean, and they knew each other's thoughts and did not speak. When it was almost dark they stopped and crouched down rather miserably under a tree stump.

'Poor kind bears!' sighed Littleflame.

'We'll try and go back and find them one day,' said Skyboy to comfort her. 'And we'll take them nice things to eat and thank them,' he added unconvincingly.

'I don't suppose we ever shall.'

Despondently they fell asleep, but only for a few minutes. Before either of them had really sunk down into the depths of sleep, two wet noses pushed under Skyboy's chin and two more under Littleflame's chin.

''Tis Cob,' said a voice.

''Tis Tob,' said another.

''Tis Nob,' said a third.

''Tis Hob,' said a fourth.

Here was a fix! Four stupid little cubs and darkness and no hope of finding the way back to the den till daylight. What a state poor Father and Mother Bear would be in! Skyboy tried to sound angry.

'You stupid bad animals!' he said severely. 'Whatever will your mother and father say!'

'Us won't never know,' said Nob and they all cuddled down together because it was the only sensible thing to do.

In the morning they tried to shoo the young bears back the way they had come, but they would not go. They tried to take them back, but they could not find the way. By the middle of the day it was obvious that they were all lost and that they would have to stay together until they could find

some high place from which they could see around them and make up their minds in which direction they should go. Never having been more than a few yards from the den in their lives, the cubs were fascinated by all the sights and smells of the wood. They scampered after butterflies and squirrels, they shinned up trees after birds, they tasted everything that they found. It was almost impossible to get them along at all. By mere chance they found the edge of the forest and the start of the tussocky plain over which the children had travelled with Father Bear, and saw the abruptly rising line of hills on the other side and the deep gash made by the mouth of the ravine. It seemed impossible now to do anything but take the cubs with them and somehow return them later to the den, but the thought of the Ollafubs in their labyrinth and the irresponsible pack of little bears made Skyboy feel very anxious and grave.

They spent one more night in the forest, grateful for the shelter of the trees, and started early next day across the plain, feeling very exposed as there were no bushes or grass taller than themselves to hide them. There were not so many things here for the cubs to chase and they made better progress, but they tired quickly and had to have a long sleep in the middle of the day. By nightfall they were still only halfway between the forest and the hills. It was cold and there was no shelter, so they decided to make a fire.

A fire was something quite new for the cubs. They brought sticks and piled them up, Skyboy struck a spark on his flint and steel, the tinder and twigs went up in a blaze and the four small bears galloped off in a fright. Then they crept back and lay watching, their eyes glowing in the firelight and their noses busy taking in the new smells. The stick fire was very hot and bright while it lasted, but it kept needing fresh fuel, as there were no big logs to be found. Soon there was nothing left but a red patch of ash which glowed and faded in the cold wind, and they curled up close together and went to sleep.

Littleflame woke up in the night feeling empty and cold. She huddled up close to the bears and lay for a while looking at the stars. An owl was calling far away in the distance and nearby she could hear a rustling noise which might have been a mouse or a dry leaf turning over in the wind. Then a stone shifted and a twig cracked. Something was moving about outside in the darkness and she lifted her head so that she could hear better. There was a faint wet snuffling going on somewhere. Her spine tingled and a cold shiver ran down her body, the snuffling stopped and all she could hear was the thumping of her own heart. She lay listening for a time, but there were no more sounds and she fell asleep again and thought no more of what she had heard in the darkness.

But in the morning, when they were searching for sticks to re-make the fire to warm themselves before starting, Skyboy gave a cry. On a soft piece of ground he had found an enormous footmark, the sort of footmark that might have been made by a giant bull with claws, and there were streaky lines where a scaly tail had been dragged along the ground. He called and they all came over to see, but as soon as the bears reached the place they bolted in different directions.

'We must get away from here quick!' said Skyboy, but it was easier said than done. They had to round up the frightened cubs and persuade them out of their hiding places, their fur standing up along their backs and making them look like frosty teasels. Hob was lying in a state of terror with his nose buried in the ground. He had to be dragged out and pulled on to his feet. Seeing him so abject made Cob and Tob and Nob ashamed and forced them to pretend to be brave.

'Turnip!' said Cob to Hob with scorn. The insult struck home and Hob went off at a gallop. They had a job to keep up with him but his wild career soon put a good distance between them and their camp. They drew breath in a hollow and it was then that Littleflame remembered what she had heard in the night.

'I mind what our Mam done tell us,' said Tob. ''Tis like t'were a Ollafub.'

'Well we've got to get on,' said Skyboy urgently, 'and we can't go by the Booming Rocks! They must have smelt us or seen us and if they know where we were last night it won't take them long to find us today. We must keep together and not waste time.'

The cubs were downcast as well as being frightened. They followed obediently when they all set off again and Hob, being the least reliable, was made to go in the middle of the line. They had nearly reached the base of the hills and were climbing a small rise. Nobody had spoken for a long time and they were all tired and thirsty and hungry. Skyboy looked back over the plain towards the bear's forest and in the middle of the expanse he saw a dark thing jumping like a monstrous grasshopper, leaping this way and then that. It looked so unnatural that he could not believe what he was seeing. He closed his eyes and rubbed them and looked again, and there was the thing still jumping, and it was jumping now along the trail over which they had come. Littleflame had seen it too.

'They're after us!' she gasped.

She seized Hob's paw and took Nob on the other side. Skyboy seized Cob and Tob. They ran trying to keep their heads down below the bushes, but the ground was rough and they were already tired out. They looked behind and they were keeping the distance between themselves and their pursuer; they had nearly reached the base of the hills where they would find rocks and trees and places to hide, when there was a deafening triumphant bellow, and a whole line of Ollafubs leaped up just in front of them. They were holding a long net and there was no escape. The children and cubs were being driven like pheasants and the leaping Ollafub behind was nothing but a decoy. They tripped and fell and lay tangled in the net, the Ollafubs closed in, rolling the net up round them, and they were caught as hopelessly as a fly is caught by a spider.

They were all so enveloped in horrible clinging net that none of them could see what happened after that. But they could feel themselves being carried deep down into the labyrinth, down steps, up slopes, round corners, scraping through narrow passages, passing through draughty echoing halls, so that all hope of ever finding a way out again seemed vain. After a very long time the nets were dumped down and unwound and shaken out. It was rather dark but they could dimly see an Ollafub's evil face, and he was grinning and smacking his lips and saying 'Haw! Haw!' Then they heard a gate clang and a key turn and soon afterwards a muffled booming told them clearly where they were.

'Are we all here?' asked Skyboy in a whisper after the booming had stopped. They all answered and crept up close to each other for comfort.

When it became light they found that they were in a large pen and the pen was closed by a barred iron gate with a padlock. It was a dirty gloomy place, there were troughs around the walls and a little light filtered in from above. Nobody came near them for hours and they were suffering greatly from hunger and thirst before a shuffling, down-at-heel, squint-eyed Ollafub staggered in with a bucket full of swill which he emptied into one of the troughs. He was not what they had expected at all, because the Ollafubs that they had so far seen were all immensely sleek and strong and bursting with vanity and good living. After emptying the bucket the Ollafub leaned up against the door post and stood looking at them with his jaw dropped, occasionally picking his teeth with a claw. He was horrid to look at and they were all frightened and apprehensive and sat without moving. After a while the Ollafub spat and said 'Cool' and whistled noisily through his front teeth. Littleflame was almost too scared to look at the creature, but she thought there would be nothing lost by being polite, so she said in a very small voice:

'Thank you for the food.'

The Ollafub leered, blew his nose into his hoof and shuffled away through the gate, locking it as he went.

'He didn't look quite so bad as the others,' said Littleflame, mightily relieved to see him go.

'Only more stupid, I think,' answered Skyboy.

They went to look at the food. It was a kind of pig swill and not very tempting, but they were all so hungry they had to try it, and they found it was just eatable but only just. The Ollafub returned with a bucket of water and put it down on the floor. He was leaning himself against the doorpost again for another good stare when heavy footsteps could be heard approaching. The Ollafub jumped through the gate, slammed and locked it and fled.

''Tisn't never only us as is scared,' whispered Tob. 'He done be scared o' somethin'.'

They ate and drank as much as they were able, then crouched in a corner dismally. The cubs had so far behaved very stoically for such young animals, but Littleflame noticed that Nob was crying. There was nothing that she could say to comfort her in their grim predicament, but she put her arms around her and cuddled her.

'I done drop my spindle!' sobbed the little bear, whose spindle was her greatest treasure.

'Never mind, Nob. If we get out—Skyboy will make you another one.' It seemed absurd to mourn a spindle just now, but it was easier perhaps to have something small and unimportant to be sad about than to think too much about what might happen to them all in a little while now that they were prisoners of the Ollafubs.

The seedy Ollafub came twice a day with swill and water, and if no one else was about he would lean against the door post and stare. Once or twice he brought the swill, leaned against the post and drank it off himself, leaving none for them. They did not mind very much, but it gave Littleflame an idea.

'I think that Ollafub is either greedy or underfed. I believe we could bribe him with food.'

'We've only got the food that he brings us, so I don't see how we could,' answered Skyboy.

'Supposing we save a little each time and store it in one of the troughs? Then we can tell him we'll give him a treat if he does something for us.'

Skyboy thought for a while. 'He certainly looks stupid enough and there's no harm in trying. But I don't quite see what he can do. If he left the gate open I don't think we'd ever find our way out. They carried us for miles and miles and all roundabout and up-over and down-through when they brought us in.'

'Well, it's better to try something than nothing and it will give us something to think about.'

So every time the swill came, they scooped a little out into another trough and they attempted too to be friendly with the weedy Ollafub.

'Can you talk?' asked Littleflame one day when he seemed to be a little less unpleasant than usual. He rolled his eyes and blew loudly and nodded his head.

'Well, do tell us your name.'

After a good deal of mouthing and tongue smacking he pronounced something that sounded like 'Nabilac'. He appeared to have a cleft palate and other speech difficulties, but they had never expected an Ollafub to be eloquent.

'It's very kind of you to bring us our food, Nabilac. Do you get enough to eat yourself?'

Nabilac rubbed his stomach mournfully and shook his head. 'Niaow!' he said.

'If we saved some up for you and gave it to you as a treat one day, would you do something for us?'

Nabilac looked frightened. He crept through the gate and looked up and down the passage and then he came back and said, 'Wha-a-at?'

'Well,' said Littleflame, not at all convinced that the plan would work. 'We're all longing to see what the passage looks like. It would be so very kind of you if you could just leave the gate unlocked for a little while one day so that we could have a little peep. It looks such a lovely passage.'

Nabilac was obviously unused to being spoken to politely. He stood smirking and turning the matter over in his small tortuous mind. Then he nodded his head and shuffled out guiltily as though he had already been caught doing something that he ought not to do.

'He do be daft,' said Cob with scorn after he had gone. 'Seein' as how he do bring in the grub 'tis him as could eat it all easy.'

They had collected nearly half a trough full of food, which they kept hidden in a corner in case Nabilac should see it and repent of his own stupidity. They decided that next day they would try out their plan. They were all dubious of its success because they felt sure that once out of the pen they would lose their way and be caught wandering round in the endless passages. They wondered why no other Ollafub had been to inspect them and why they had been left so long. The daily booming from the cauldrons never let them forget the sinister fate for which they were intended.

And that very evening, another Ollafub did come and he was quite a different kind of Ollafub from wretched Nabilac. Nabilac came with him and was crawling on the ground behind him, licking his hoofs with a long blue tongue. The second Ollafub was huge and sleek and he cracked his tail like a whip. He made the children and cubs line up in front of him and he looked at them in disgust.

'No dam good for broth even!' he growled angrily. 'A poor job you've made of it!' and he kicked Nabilac, who flattened himself even flatter.

The big Ollafub stalked out angrily and the gate was slammed and the key was turned, but his visit had an unexpected result. He was so disgusted at the scrawny objects he had seen in the larder that stop-gap supplies were ordered in and that afternoon there was pandemonium down the passage as a herd of pigs was driven in. Poor Nabilac was almost frantic and his task was not an enviable one. The pigs were squealing and running in all directions and a herd of pigs scattered through a labyrinth took a great deal of collecting, and when he finally slammed the gate on the last one, not even Littleflame could have persuaded him then to leave the padlock undone. The pen had become a bedlam. The excited pigs tore round and round, they bit each other and squealed, they pretended to be frightened of bears and squealed some more, there was nowhere to sit down, hardly anywhere to stand up, then to cap it all they found the trough of food which was being saved for Nabilac and gobbled everything up in an instant. The disappointment was almost more than the children and cubs could bear. They felt that the sooner they were popped in the booming cauldrons and finished off the better.

But it was Hob who brought a tiny ray of hope back into their despairing minds. For some days he had been trying to make friends with a mouse who used to come in under the iron gate after the swill had been brought to find little pickings on the floor. Hob used to save little bits and scatter them about and when the mouse had eaten its fill, it would run back under the gate to its hole in the passage. Today Hob was taking no notice of the pigs but was crouching up against the gate looking hard at something on the ground just out of reach outside. The mouse was sitting on the other side of the gate looking at Hob.

''Tis Hob as done give you all that there lovely grub,' Hob was saying. 'Do'ee pull it a teeny bit, do'ee now!'

The mouse put its head on one side and looked at the insignificant wisp of wool on the floor beside it.

'Gin 'ee kin fetch it,' tis Hob as'll give 'ee a girt scrummy feast,' Hob cajoled, holding out a horrid little lump of swill on his paw.

The mouse looked at the swill and made up its mind. It dropped on to its four very small feet and started to drag the wool along the floor towards Hob. As soon as it was within reach Hob stretched out his paw through the bars and took it and pulled. It was the woollen yarn off Nob's spindle. He twisted it carefully round one of the iron bars and handed the mouse the swill. The mouse ran off to its hole and with unaccustomed boldness Hob pushed his way back through the herd of pigs.

''Tis us as kin git out if us kin git out the gate!' he exclaimed excitedly.

'What do you mean, Hob?' asked Skyboy, hoping that what he said was more sensible than it sounded.

Hob tried to explain but he was too excited, so he pulled Skyboy over to the gate and showed him the yarn. Skyboy stood looking at it and thinking—IF the yarn held—IF they

could get through this gate and follow the yarn——.
There were a lot of 'if's' but very exciting possibilities. Skyboy and Hob pushed their way back through the pigs.

'Do you know where you dropped your spindle, Nob?'
asked Skyboy.

Tears came to Nob's eyes. She still mourned her spindle.

'I done drop it when they done cotch us. I were that
scared,' she said.

Skyboy explained Hob's discovery to the others and they
decided on desperate measures. Nabilac was so frightened
of the pigs that he brought no food for them that evening
and they were battling and squealing and wild with hunger
by next day. With great difficulty the children and cubs
pushed their way to the gate and stood holding the bars to
keep on their feet while the pigs fought and jostled all
round them. When Nabilac came down the passage swinging two great buckets of swill, pandemonium broke out.
He was hardly able to open the gate, and the children
cheered and encouraged him and helped him to push his
way in. Once there, he disappeared immediately with his
buckets under a sea of ravenous pigs. The children and cubs
slipped through the open gate. Skyboy seized the end of
Nob's yarn and running it through his fingers he set off
down the passage, followed by the others. It said a lot for
Nob's spinning that everywhere the yarn held and led them
unerringly up and down and round and through until they
dashed headlong through the entrance and out into the open
air. The sky was black and a flurry of rain met them as they
ran. They knew that the danger was not over. Nabilac was
bound to give chase and the terrible noise made by the pigs
would warn the other Ollafubs that something was wrong,
but to be running in the open through the pelting rain was
a wonderful feeling after their long miserable confinement
and their spirits rose at once.

The entrance through which they had escaped opened out of the rocks at the base of the hills on to the tussocky plain and they were running now along the edge of the plain below the hills. They passed the mouth of the ravine, panted up an incline and paused for a moment to look back. As they looked, something exploded with a great bellow from the entrance and went leaping off over the plain rattling two empty buckets and pursued by a squealing horde of furious pigs. It was Nabilac. He leaped into the distance running for his life and the pigs scattered in all directions.

But that was not the serious part of the pursuit. Almost immediately on his heels came the big fat Ollafubs leaping out of the doorway, first in ones and twos and then in groups and crowds, roaring and bellowing and brandishing their monstrous spoons. There hardly seemed a chance of escape before all those infuriated monsters, but the children and cubs were turning to struggle on again when suddenly from the mouth of the ravine broke an enormous wall of water, falling in a great curtain of foam and lights, sweeping everything in front of it, picking up the Ollafubs like a lot of pebbles and carrying them in a great irresistible flood far away across the plain.

You must be as bewildered as the children were when they saw that great cascade of water spangled with lights pouring out of the ravine and sweeping their enemies away into the distance, so I shall have to go back and tell you what Thunder did after he had lost sight and sound of the children when they were picking raspberries among the Booming Rocks.

The first thing that he did was to head the sheep and goats for home. Both flocks had wise leaders and he knew that they would be safe. Then he raced down through the trees to the Booming Rocks, and it did not take him long to find the baskets of raspberries hidden under the wall, the torn bits of clothes in the gully and the bears' footprints at the bottom of the ravine. He knew that bear and as soon as he found his footprints mixed up with the marks made by the children he was content. He also knew exactly why the rocks boomed and that they boomed regularly every day, not only when the wind blew. All the wind did was sometimes to carry the sound to the village. But it was no good telling the people, they were pig-headed and forgetful and preferred their own theories, so he had kept his knowledge to himself.

As soon as he was assured that the children were safe he started to search around among the Booming Rocks. The Ollafubs were old enemies of his. He had known the time long years ago when they had swarmed over the countryside destroying the villages, eating up the flocks and herds and spoiling everything that they came across. There had been great battles and finally the Ollafubs had been beaten back and driven underground into this labyrinth, but the danger remained that their numbers might increase and that they might break out again on their paths of destruction. It was one of Thunder's self-imposed tasks to keep an eye on the Booming Rocks.

He came to the entrance with the kitchen middens at either side where the children had seen the Ollafub come up to cool himself. The vultures were back and the cooking smell was very strong. He slid down the gully where they had been caught by Father Bear and trotted along to the window in the side of the ravine. He pulled himself up and lay along a ledge and for a long time he watched. The Ollafubs had finished their meal and were lying in sodden heaps along the walls. Some were snoring, some were sucking bones, some were drinking from great flagons. The cauldrons had been pulled off the fires and the cooks were finishing the scraps. The more Thunder looked, the more his hackles rose and the less he liked it. After a while he slipped silently off the ledge and turned up the ravine in the opposite direction from that which the children had taken. It was evening but he went on steadily up and up and up right into the heart of the mountains and although it grew quite dark he did not hesitate because he was sure of the way.

High up and far beyond the farthest place where men ever brought their flocks in summer, there was a cave which was the home of a powerful fairy race called the Tungi People. Hardly anything was known about them and nobody had ever seen them, but you could tell that they were there because of the lights they carried. Inside the cave was a lake of clear water, and the Tungi People lived on the walls and ceiling of the cave, and their lights were reflected in the water. So if you had gone into the cave you might have thought that you were floating by night in interstellar space, so surrounded you would have been by stars.

At the time when there had been the great battles with the Ollafubs, the Tungi People had fought against them, and it was partly due to their power that the Ollafubs had been beaten and driven underground. They were so terrible and mysterious in the way they did things that if Thunder had been alone he would have been afraid to come here, but he had a friend who often came here too and he hoped to find him.

His friend was an old man who looked like a hermit and whose name was Cottonshirt. When Cottonshirt was tired he would come to this place among the mountains and sit at the entrance to the cave and he would sit there for a very long time and watch the stream which ran out of the cave fall in a shining arc into the ravine below. If the sun shone a rainbow would play in the spray and a white falcon would soar in circles round the waterfall and a fine mist would blow back against the rocks and sprinkle the mountain flowers that grew there. Sometimes Cottonshirt would go into the cave and speak with the Tungi People and as soon as he felt refreshed and well again, he would leave the cave and the waterfall and go down the mountain and nobody would hear of him again for years.

When Thunder reached the cave he looked in and he saw Cottonshirt sitting cross-legged on the lake and there was an arc of fire over him and all the lights were shining. Thunder lay down and waited and when Cottonshirt came out it was morning and they greeted each other like old friends. They did not need to say very much because Cottonshirt had already guessed why Thunder had come. He knew his troubles of old and the Tungi People had guessed too because the lights were shifting restlessly to and fro across the water and there was an electric feeling of anger in the air.

'There are far too many of them down by the Booming Rocks,' said Thunder. 'They have grown fat and proud again. The old troubled times will return if we don't rout them out.'

'The Tungi People know and they are growing angry again,' answered Cottonshirt. 'This time they will fight them with water and storms. All you need do is to wait.'

'Will you fight with us?' asked Thunder, feeling the deep growling excitement rising up inside him and remembering the battles he had fought in before.

Cottonshirt was silent for a long time, then he said: 'No. Anger has gone out of me. I no longer fight. Even Ollafubs can rouse compassion and that would be no help.'

They sat without saying anything and then Cottonshirt rose.

'I have been here long enough,' he said. 'I have got work to do.'

He said goodbye to Thunder, who lay and watched him disappear down the mountain path. He knew it was no good asking him where he was going, he never told that to anybody.

So Thunder just stayed there and waited while the lights behind him in the cave grew more and more restless and lightning flashed on the horizon and storm clouds were conjured into the sky. He saw the lightning grow into jagged sheets of flame and the sky became black like a pit, and then the rain started, and what rain it was! So fierce and relentless that you could not see through its grey curtain, and the waterfall became a torrent and the ravine was filled with roaring. Lights came out of the cave and there was a ghostly boat on the water manned by lights and Thunder got into the boat and the wind streamed through his hair so that he looked like a grey wraith gliding down in midstream where the water gleamed like moving silk between the lacy turbulence of its edges.

Lights were everywhere and the torrent rose and rose until it nearly filled the valley and he was soaring down between the mountains as an eagle might have soared, only instead of being on wings in the air he was on a great wall of water which was being squeezed and constricted between the narrowing rocks so that now its pace was almost at a standstill and it was rising steadily upwards while the boat circled round and round as the eagle might have circled before he swooped.

They had reached the Booming Rocks and Thunder could hear the gulch and gurgle of the water as it swept through the labyrinth and clouds of hissing steam went up from the hall of the cauldrons. Then suddenly the end of the ravine was before them and the wall of water burst from the narrow entrance carrying everything before it, throwing a wreckage of rocks, trees, cauldrons, spoons and terrified Ollafubs in a tidal wave across the plain.

The children and the bear cubs were still crouching on the rise from which they had watched the extraordinary rout of their enemies and they were still feeling dazed and unable to believe that all that had happened had been true. Nobody knew how Thunder had safely ridden the flood or why the water which had risen to their feet had receded before touching them, leaving a tide mark of torn leaves and branches as it went. The Tungi People had done their work well and now they were rising like sparks from a birchwood fire and disappearing into the sky.

'One thing puzzles me,' said Skyboy after the awed silence had been broken, explanations made and both sides of the story told. 'What would have happened if we'd still been inside the labyrinth when the water came down?'

'Us'd of been drownded wet as wet,' said Cob.

'The Tungi People know more than we do,' said Thunder, who was lying at their feet looking just like an ordinary dog.

'They must have found out before they came down,' said Littleflame wonderingly. 'I wish we had seen them.'

Suddenly Hob cried out: 'Squeeze our paws if it isn't never our Mam an' Ole Pad a comin' to git us!' He rolled himself into a ball and hid his face between his paws.

Sure enough, two burly shapes were rolling along over the plain, picking their way among the rocks and the broken cauldrons left high and dry by the flood. The three other cubs watched apprehensively. When Mother and Father Bear reached the place where they all were sitting they threw down a great bundle they were carrying and grunted. Then Father Bear walked up to the cubs and gave each one a clout on the side of its head; then he walked up to the children and did the same. Then he grunted again and that was all. The punishment was over and bears do not carry grudges.

The bundle caused great excitement and joy. In it were all the bears' possessions including the tossers.

'''Tis powerful boggy yon,' said Father Bear. 'Us'll bide here.'

It is hard to tell what delight was caused by this good news. After surviving such adventures together the children and the bear cubs did not want to part.

'Were *all* the Ollafubs drowned?' asked Littleflame, looking out over the plain.

'Ollafubs are never *all* drowned,' answered Thunder. 'They find more caves to hide in and some of them are always left to come out later on.'

# On picking up a Baby

After their escape from the Ollafubs it was some time before Skyboy and Littleflame would venture far from the village. Skyboy was happy carving his wooden pipes. He had a whole collection of them, one for each mood and he kept them stuck round his belt and was always making new ones. Littleflame would sit near him, whirling the fluffy wool on to her spindle until it was full of yarn or fashioning clay dollies out of mud. But often she would get impatient, longing for something more active to do, even for another adventure. So one restless spring morning she went off to look for the bear cubs.

Tob was the only one at home and he seemed even more preoccupied than Skyboy, he scarcely seemed to see or hear her. On a sandy patch outside the den he was drawing triangles; he had a home-made measuring rod marked with notches and a line of sticks standing upright in the ground. He was hurrying backwards and forwards between the drawings and the sticks, measuring this and measuring that, muttering to himself and stopping every now and then to count upon his paws. Then he became immensely pleased and excited, tossed his measuring rod into the air and did a little dance of joy all round his apparatus, ending up with a happy somersault which landed him in front of Littleflame.

'Whatever are you doing, Tob, which makes you so awfully pleased?'

Tob looked at her with his head on one side, trying to collect his wits. The pale rings round his eyes made him look very wise.

'Our Mam'd be cross if she knowed,' he said. ''Tis dinner as I did oughter find.'

'What is it you are doing instead of finding dinner?'

'I were learnin' myself to measure things if they be tall or little,' answered Tob.

'What sort of things?'

'Trees an' mountains an' such—them things as do have shadows.'

'Whatever for?'

''Tis to find if they be big or little.' Tob stood scratching his head and looking puzzled.

'But why? Tall trees have honey in them or little stumps have honey in them and everything has shadows and the shadows are longer in the morning and the evening than in the middle of the day.'

''Tis so! 'Tis so!' cried Tob excitedly and started to dance round his sticks and his drawings again.

'Do stop dancing and sit down,' said Littleflame, feeling rather cross with him. 'Measuring things is just stupid. I want to know if you have found out any more about the Tungi People.'

Tob sat down obediently and tried to bring his mind back from the problems that were so besetting him.

'Them as wasn't never there 'cept for the lights?' he asked rather vaguely.

'Yes, that's them,' said Littleflame. 'Do you know where they live or what they are?'

'Them's the Tungi People what near drownded all them Ollafubs.'

'Oh, Tob, you are stupid! I don't believe you are thinking at all! I want to know more about them—I know all that already.'

Tob scratched his head and looked unhappy.

'I do be thinkin',' he answered humbly. ''Tis rare hard to be thinkin' o' two things at once't.'

'Never mind, Tob,' said Littleflame, who could not help smiling at his solemn anxious face. 'I'll come back and ask you another day.'

So she left Tob to his measuring and wandered off through the woods, thinking that bears and boys were boring and unsatisfactory. And she came to the banks of a stream which wandered between clumps of alder and willow on the edge of the cultivated lands, and when she saw the stream she suddenly had an idea. If she could not find out any more about the Tungi People, she would play at being the Tungi People and see what it was like. She would make a boat, she would have lights, she would go down the water, she might even find a waterfall and go over the top.

Now she was happy and busy and her head was full of ideas. She searched around for straight pieces of wood and bound them into a frame with long withies from the willow trees. She filled the gaps with dry reeds and tied it all securely together. She dug clay from the bank with her hands and made four little lamps shaped like shallow jugs, each with a lip to hold a wick. She looked about for wisps of sheep's wool caught on the thorns and twisted them into wicks and ran back to the village to beg a little jar of oil from her grandmother for the lamps and a big flat loaf of bread for herself. She had a tinderbox of her own and when she returned to her boat she poured the oil into the lamps, soaked the wicks and set them alight. She placed one lamp at each corner of the boat and pushed it off from the shore. When it was well afloat, she climbed in and settled herself cross-legged in the middle.

'One boat,' she thought, 'and five little flames.'

She held up her hands with the fingers outstretched as though they were being blown back like the real flames of the lamps; the breeze lifted her hair and blew it back too and down the river went the five little flames, now turned into ten little flames as the smooth water caught the reflections in the evening light.

Concentration on her play made Littleflame forget all about time and distance. Only when she grew hungry and it was almost dark did she start looking about for a place where she could land and start her return. But mist had come down on the water and the stream seemed to have no banks, only sometimes she passed a ghostly clump of bulrushes or the flat leaves of water weeds floating on the surface. The air was still and silent and the boat moved imperceptibly so that the flames of the lamps rose upright and she altered her fingers to match. She floated on and on, and gradually darkness and mist swallowed her up; only the four lamps went on burning steadily, their four reflections following obediently, broken a little by the ripple on the surface of the water.

Night passed in a trance-like dream and dawn came dank and cold as only dawn on water can be. The thick mist lifted and there in front of her was the morning star piercing the river with a shivering golden spear. She reached out to catch it, but it eluded her, trembling just out of reach, and she was afraid to lean too far for fear of upsetting the boat and tumbling in. All at once, there was a great commotion around her, splashing, quacking and whirring of wings.

## On Picking up a Baby

The boat rocked violently, the lamps pitched overboard and Littleflame was only just able to stop herself going after them. She had floated into the middle of a flock of ducks who had taken fright and now were whirring round above her head calling out to each other, their pinions whistling in the half-darkness. She crouched down listening to their wings; then there was a grating sound as the boat bumped and ground along the bottom and came to a stop. She could see reeds and a tree, but it was not light enough yet to land. She huddled up against the cold and waited for daylight, hungrily chewing one end of her loaf.

The boat had run aground on a marshy promontory and as soon as she could see clearly, Littleflame pushed it in among the reeds, making it as secure as possible so that it would not float away. Then she splashed through the tussocks and shallow water till she reached firm ground. There was a big gaunt tree nearby with a split trunk which she noted carefully so that she could remember where the boat was hidden, but it was difficult to see much else because of the thick pale grass which was taller than herself. She pushed her way through and came to a group of thorn trees, up one of which she scrambled to get a better view. She lay along a flat branch, gnawing at her loaf, looking out around her and wondering what she should do.

Behind where the boat lay, the water looked more like a lake than a river. It was wide and shallow with islands of reeds and tall grass, and there were flocks of water birds swimming on the surface or wading on the edges. In front of her was a wide expanse of the tall pale grass, more trees and a line of low blue hills. Playing at being the Tungi People had quite gone out of her head. It had not turned out at all as she had expected and now she had to find some way of getting home again. To return by boat would be very difficult as she would have to punt all the way against the

43

stream. Perhaps it would be better to abandon the boat and follow the water's edge on foot, but seeing the long tangled grass and the swampy patches, she did not think that this would be easy either.

She was turning these things over in her mind when she heard a curious sound in the distance. At first it was very faint and she had to stop chewing her bread to hear it at all. Then it grew louder and seemed to be approaching at a steady pace, a curious rhythmic chanting—'Ai! Ai! Ai!— Ai! Ai! Ai!'—accompanied by tinkling and the steady thump of bare feet on trodden earth. Now it was loud and near and suddenly from between two clumps of tall grass appeared a woman dressed in a long blue scarf and a wide red skirt, jogging along at a steady trot, her ankles and wrists loaded with tinkling bracelets and a great black bundle balanced on her head. After her came another woman dressed just the same, and another and another, all carrying bundles on their heads, all jogging along at the same pace and all chanting as they went—'Ai! Ai! Ai!— Ai! Ai! Ai!——'

Their path passed right under the tree from which Littleflame was watching and she stared open-mouthed at the strange procession hurrying along underneath her. After the women had passed there was a gap, then a line of lean, long-legged men with blue scarves wrapped round their heads and nothing much else on at all. They were carrying hatchets and picks and ropes and an assortment of curious tools and they ran silently, only thumping with their big splay feet. Then there was disorder as a leaping herd of small white goats chased by a crowd of wild little boys and girls rushed by in confusion, followed by a pack of lurcher dogs, their pink tongues lolling.

When the last one had passed, and the chanting and tinkling and bleating and barking were fading into the distance, Littleflame slipped down out of her tree and trotted after them. All thoughts of returning home had gone. She had never seen anything like these strange people before and she was brimming over with curiosity.

She did not have to follow far, for soon she heard the noises in front of her change, the chanting and tinkling and thumping stopped, there was a lot more bleating and barking and shouting, and when she came out on to a clear space of short grass on the edge of a wood, she found that the strange people were busy making a kind of camp. Two big crackling fires were already burning, the women were sitting round in a circle untying their enormous black bundles and the men were jumping around with their tools, feverishly turning over stones and logs, grubbing holes and dabbling in puddles, catching beetles and frogs and snakes and popping them straight into cooking pots. The dogs and children were driving the goats towards the wood where they could feed on the fresh green leaves.

Littleflame had only just stepped out on to the short grass when the lurcher dogs saw her. They left the goats and came racing towards her, growling and barking terribly. She was not a particularly brave little girl, but she was not at all afraid of dogs. She stood perfectly still and when they were right up round her in a circle, growling horribly with their white teeth bared, she said sternly:

'Be quiet! All of you!'

Then she took the rest of her loaf and divided it into just so many pieces as there were dogs, gave one piece to each dog and marched boldly into the camp with all the dogs following meekly with their tails down.

She was greeted with cries of astonishment and soon the strange people were crowding round her, touching her hair and skin and feeling her clothes. They were not at all un-friendly, only very inquisitive, and the ones who were nearby shouted to the ones farther off, so soon she was surrounded by the whole tribe, laughing and chattering in a strange tongue. They looked like gypsies, with black eyes and black hair and dark skin, and she came to call them to herself the 'Snake Gypsies', as many of the men had dead snakes hung round their waists or dead snakes strung on sticks, and the food that was being cooked consisted largely of snakes.

After a tremendous hubbub in which everybody had to touch her at least once and everybody had to make excited comments, they all started to disperse again to their various jobs, the men to make up the fires and catch more creatures to put in the stews, the women to unpack their bundles, out of which came the strangest mixture of belongings, pots and pans, shoes, lumps of bread, bunches of wild garlic, clothes and shells and trinkets and children—scores of squirming brown babies with nothing on at all. The babies seemed to know their business just like everybody else and instead of demanding attention from their mothers, they all started playing with stones and twigs, or squabbling and pulling each other's hair, or laughing and tumbling about together. There seemed to be no telling which baby belonged to which mother and they all looked exactly alike, but they seemed very happy and were soon in a tangled brown heap. Littleflame sat on the edge of the heap and almost at once became the middle of the heap as they scrambled all over her, delighted to find something new to play with.

Snakes, frogs, beetles, garlic, all were being thrown together into the cooking pots and soon a strong smell of food arose and filled the air. The women were kneading coarse flour into dough which they wrapped round hot stones and left in long rows on the ground to bake. When the bread was ready, they broke it off the stones and piled it in heaps, the cooking pots were taken off the fires and the gypsies squatted round in a circle scooping the stew up with pieces of bread which acted as rough spoons. The mothers fed the children and signed to Littleflame to join in the meal. She did not feel tempted by the snake stew but found the bread good and very satisfying.

The meal had been enormous and afterwards no one seemed inclined to move. Most of them lay, swollen like boa constrictors, their hands over their stomachs, their big flat feet sticking up like gravestones. Littleflame, who had not eaten so much as the others, had time to look closely at their bracelets and their anklets and their bright-coloured clothes. The lurcher dogs moved about among the prostrate people and finished all the scraps and licked all the cooking pots clean. The goats browsed among the bushes and soon everybody slept.

Littleflame awoke with a start and looked around her. In her dreams she had been trotting along with the gypsy women chanting 'Ai! Ai! Ai!—Ai! Ai! Ai!——' just as they did and carrying something very heavy on her head. Her legs were too short and gradually they had drawn away from her and she could hear their chanting and thumping fading away into the distance. And there must have been something of reality in the dream because when she woke there was not a gypsy left in the camp that she could see, not a dog, not a child, not even a goat. They had all gone chanting and tinkling and thumping away into the night and left her all alone. She felt sad and a little hurt that nobody had said good-bye or woken her up to tell her that they were going, but perhaps it was not surprising, seeing what queer, wild creatures they were. She got up and started to search around in case any bread had been left, but there was not a scrap of anything, the lurcher dogs had seen to that. The camp had been left like all gypsy camps, a rag here, a cracked cooking pot there, one shoe forlornly on its face, a dropped anklet, a bunch of garlic pitched into a bush. She was about to turn away from the slovenly, much-trodden site when she heard a little cry coming from behind a clump of grass. She pushed her way through searching, and there, rather forlorn and without a stitch of clothing, lay one of the gypsy babies, playing sadly with its own fingers. Littleflame stared and the baby stared back.

'Well, that's carelessness if you like!' exclaimed Littleflame indignantly. 'They're in too much of a hurry even to pick up all their babies!'

She felt sure that the gypsies would never come back to find the baby, she doubted if they even knew how many babies they had, she doubted if they could even count. She could not leave the baby to die of cold and hunger, so she leaned down and picked the poor little thing up in her arms and tucked it inside her tunic. She would follow the trail of the Snake Gypsies as fast as she could and return the baby to its mother, or anyhow to one of its mothers if she could not find the right one.

The baby seemed pleased to snuggle inside her clothes and she propped him as best she could on her hip and searched around to find the path which the gypsies had taken. This was easy enough, as the multitude of bare feet and goats' hoofs all following in a line had beaten out a firm road which was clear to follow. She jogged along, trying to imitate the rhythm of the strange people for the benefit of the baby and sometimes starting up an 'Ai! Ai! Ai!——' to make him feel less strange. He stared up at her from his seat with large opaque black eyes.

At midday the sun grew hot and Littleflame sat down to rest on a fallen tree stump. She was both hungry and thirsty but so anxious to catch up with the Snake Gypsies and hand over her charge that she would not allow herself time to look for food. But as soon as she stopped moving, the baby let out a heart-rending wail.

'Poor little thing,' she thought. 'He must be hungry.'

She gave him her fingers to suck, but these did not comfort him for long and she found the only way to keep him quiet was to keep moving. She was climbing a stony slope and had to pause for breath; at each pause the baby wailed, and then when she started off again and he was quiet, she thought she could hear an answering wail in the distance. She reached the top of the slope and, jogging the baby up and down to keep him silent, she listened again and, sure enough, a voice was following them. Disregarding the baby's protests she sat down by the side of the trail, waiting to find out what was coming after them, hoping that it was not another lost baby who would want to be carried on the other hip.

It was a baby, but not the kind of baby she had feared and not a baby alone but a baby accompanied by a heaven-sent mother. Her own baby had abandoned himself to a tempest of roaring when round a bend in the track appeared first a skipping kid, then an anxious long-bearded nanny-goat. Littleflame welcomed them with delight and blessed this further proof of the fecklessness of the Snake Gypsies, who not only left their children behind but their goats and kids as well.

Nothing more welcome than a nanny-goat could have appeared in that wilderness and she seemed to know exactly what was expected of her. She lay down on her side and suckled the gypsy baby until he was so full that he fell off like an inflated tick. Then the kid had a turn and there was enough milk left for Littleflame, who squeezed it out into the wooden bowl she always carried and drank it gratefully.

They all felt much happier now, the baby because he was full fed, the goats because they had at last caught up with somebody and Littleflame because there was now a motherly old goat with whom she could share her worries. They journeyed along together, secure in each other's company and warmed by each other at night, but it was not until the middle of the following day that they came across the first gypsy encampment with its burnt-out fires and jettisoned belongings. Littleflame searched over the trodden ground, hoping to find something edible or useful, but hoping too that she would not find any more lost babies. She did find a half-burned loaf wrapped round a stone, which had been overlooked by the dogs. She broke it off and took it back to share with the old goat.

'No, my dear,' said the goat kindly. 'I can find plenty of leaves and grass. Eat half of it now, my darling, and keep the rest for tomorrow.'

'We are travelling much more slowly than the gypsies,' said Littleflame sadly. 'They left their camp not this morning, but yesterday morning, so we are now more than a day behind them.'

'Comfort yourself, my precious and count your blessings,' answered the goat. 'Summer's coming and things might be a lot worse.'

It would be dull to follow every stage of their journey. They went through grassland and woodland, up hill and down hill, over dry ground and over wet ground, and it became more obvious each day that the Snake Gypsies were getting farther and farther ahead and, try as they might, they soon felt that there was very little prospect of catching them up at all unless something very unexpected happened. Littleflame lay awake at night knowing that she would soon have to make a decision whether to pursue the elusive gypsies in the hope that they would settle down somewhere for a few days and rest from their hectic journey, or to turn back on the wearisome road home with her queerly assorted companions.

## On Picking up a Baby

The old goat, whose name was Nannilinka, took life as it came, was happy to stay, was happy to go, was pleased to feed them all on her warm milk, was pleased to cuddle them on cold nights, was always cheerful and hopeful. Kiddilinka, her child, had the same optimistic nature, although she was volatile and unpredictable and wore herself out by jumping and running much farther than she need. Littleflame had asked the old goat what the baby was called and Nannilinka had rolled him over and studied him carefully.

'A lot of them looked just like this,' she said, 'but——' —and again she examined him from head to toe—'I *think* this one is "Intelligent Edible Frog".'

'What a name!' exclaimed Littleflame. 'I can't possibly call him all that! It's far too long and quite absurd. Let's call him Tadpole and be done with it!' So Tadpole he became for that journey at any rate.

They had been hurrying all day up and down a series of small rocky hills covered with thorn bushes, monotonous country where one hill was exactly like the next and the stones rolled uncomfortably underfoot. Littleflame's sandals had worn out long ago, but by searching each gypsy camp as they passed through, she had managed to pick up a number of odd shoes, and although they had at first all been right-footed, at last she found a left-footed one to complete a pair. But they did not fit comfortably and all that day Tadpole had seemed terribly heavy. He was thriving on so much goat's milk and beginning to grow quite fat. He seemed content to jog along all day and did not mind how much he was bumped and shaken, but when he was put down in the evening, he became fractious and difficult. He missed the other babies and Kiddilinka jumped and ran too fast to make a good companion for him. Sometimes he just sat and bawled with his mouth wide open and no tears coming from his screwed-up eyes. Nannilinka would tickle him with her beard and make sympathetic bleating noises, but he only grew angrier and bawled louder.

'It's no good,' sighed Littleflame, beginning to despair of this hopeless journey. 'We shall never catch his mother up and whatever shall we do with him? He doesn't really seem to like any of us very much, or if he does, he doesn't show it!'

'Keep your heart up, little treasure,' encouraged Nannilinka. 'I'll think of something. Perhaps we could catch some of the animal messengers who pass close by here. They might help. I used to be one myself, so I don't mind asking.'

'Who are the animal messengers?' asked Littleflame.

'Oh, just animals who carry the animal news. They scatter it as they go for the other animals to pick up and read. Donkeys do it round about here, I've been reading their signs and picking up their news as I trot along the trail. When you see dogs snuffling about in the early mornings, that's what they're doing—just picking up the news, and that's what eagles are doing when you see them soaring high up among the clouds, and that's what fishes are doing when you see them nosing in among the wet stones.'

'Oh,' said Littleflame and considered for a while. 'What sort of things do they want to know?' she asked, thinking how little she really understood about the world.

'All animals are different,' answered Nannilinka. 'Dogs want to know about bones and other dogs and the king and queen dogs in far-off countries. Horses want to know about galloping grounds and sweet hay. Birds want to know about storms and winds and little rocky islands in cold shining water far away in the north where nobody ever comes. Eels want to know about drowned carcasses and combed seaweed and the sharp taste of salt water where the rivers run out into the sea. It is all there to read if you know how.'

Nannilinka went off, apparently to browse among the

bushes, but perhaps to read her own particular bits of news. Littleflame wondered what goats would be interested in— cliffs to climb perhaps and bark to chew and other goats to keep them company.

She was roused next morning by a deafening noise above her head. At first she thought that Tadpole was bellowing into her ear, but it was something even louder than Tadpole.

'Hee haw! Hee haw! Hee Haw!' it went and she looked up to see a donkey standing over her with a half-grown foal by its side. Kiddilinka was jumping round in great excitement and Nannilinka was wagging her beard and looking very pleased with herself.

'No more walking on poor tired feet, my darling,' she said proudly. 'Now you can ride like a queen! The donkeys will carry us as far as the plain, where the horses will take us over, and then the camels, until we really do catch up with those tiresome gypsy people. Cheer up, my dearie, forget your troubles. If Nannilinka can't help, who can?'

The donkeys were in a hurry to get off and stamped and brayed impatiently while Tadpole and Kiddilinka were fed and Littleflame got her bowlful. Then off they all scurried across the stony ground, the little hoofs beating out a sharp tattoo while Tadpole clung like a brown leech to the broad woolly back in front of Littleflame.

'Huddi-tutti, huddi-tutti . . .' went the hoofs, and if bones were not broken, they were certainly bruised and shaken. But they made a good pace with Nannilinka picking out the way and Kiddilinka and the young donkey frisking in the rear. They passed through three deserted gypsy camps that day and another in the morning of the second day, when the donkeys put them down and they were immediately re-mounted on two beautiful cream-coloured ponies. This time Kiddilinka was put up too, much to her indignation.

'Are they leaving messages all this time?' shouted Littleflame as they galloped off over the wide plain, but her voice was lost between the wind and the drumming hoofs.

'Blockety block, blockety block, blockety block . . .' went the horses and they threw up their heads and snorted and their manes streamed out behind their proud heads and the ground flew by from under them. The plain ran out into sandhills and they had hardly time to thank the horses when they were up on two tall camels and striding out into a desert of sand. This time even Nannilinka was riding. The camels moved like ships in a sea swell and the pale waves of sand swept back behind them and the hot sun beat down and drained all colour from the earth so that everything was glaring dusty uniform whitish-grey.

Littleflame felt desperately sick and uncomfortable, but she knew that they could never have crossed this awful desert without help. She was grateful to the camels, but wished that they would be more friendly.

'Why are they so disdainful and proud?' she managed to ask between the sickening lurches of their progress.

'They know a secret from the beginning of the world and they've kept it a secret ever since. Hold tight, my darling, and mind how you go or you'll be slipping off the stern and once overboard they'd be far too proud to stop and pick you up.'

Littleflame clung desperately to the camel's curls and clutched Tadpole in anguish, wondering how she could ever survive this part of the journey.

'Bismillah . . . Bismillah . . . Bismillah!'

The camels strode on over the monotonous dry sea to the monotonous accompaniment of their own supercilious thoughts.

Then suddenly they saw the Snake Gypsies in front of them, and the extraordinary thing was that they were all upside down and running on their heads, and underneath them was a city all upside down as well with its domes and spires and rooftops floating above a shining lake. Soon they could hear the 'Ai! Ai! Ai! . . .' of the women and the bleating of the goats and the barking of the lurcher dogs. As soon as that happened, Nannilinka and Kiddilinka were off the camels' backs and racing across the sand in two small clouds of dust, and Tadpole began to jump and shout in a most alarming way.

They drew closer and suddenly the gypsies jumped upright again and started running on their feet instead of on their heads with the city above and beyond them and the lake turned into the sky. The camels strode on without changing their pace or changing their expressions until they were abreast of the gypsies and right in the middle of the barking and the bleating. Littleflame slipped thankfully to the ground, still clutching a struggling Tadpole, the gypsies closed round her chattering excitedly, a young woman in a scarlet skirt seized the baby and danced off with him, swirling her skirt delightedly. Bundles were off-loaded, everybody talked at once, the camels strode off scornfully, there was so much noise and confusion Littleflame could scarcely realize that her mission had ended at last and that Tadpole had been returned safely to his own people.

The Snake Gypsies made their camp where they were and set about their usual tasks with more than their usual clamour. Snakes were captured, beetles collected, fires lighted and a great feast prepared in honour of Tadpole's return. In fact, they were so pleased and excited it was impossible to imagine why they had abandoned him so neglectfully before. Nannilinka took Littleflame to visit the other goats, who bleated over her approvingly and gave her all the warm milk that she could drink. She asked them why no one had gone back for Tadpole. They shook their beards and confabulated together.

## On Picking up a Baby

'They hasn't ever learned to go backwards,' announced one wise old Nanny gravely.

'But they could have turned round and gone back forwards.'

''Tisn't in nature to go back forwards. Why, you'd have to turn your feet round, child!'

The goats seemed so positive about this that Littleflame did not argue. She felt that they were rather stupid and that the gypsies were rather ungrateful, because nobody ever really thanked her for returning Tadpole and she was not even sure that she ever saw him again unless he was the owner of one of the legs or arms protruding from the bundle of squirming babies. She was dreadfully tired after her long journey and so relieved that she was no longer responsible for Tadpole that although the gypsies were kind and pressed food on her and gave her blankets to sit on, soon her head drooped and her eyes closed and she was hardly aware of what was going on around her.

The gypsies sat up far into the night beating out their happiness on the upturned cooking pots and jumping up in twos and threes to do crazy impromptu dances in the firelight. The lurcher dogs sat round in a ring, their eyes reflecting the firelight and glowing out of the darkness. Whenever the noise got more than they could bear, they howled mournfully, long quavering unhappy howls passing from one dog to the next all round the circle. Nobody slept except Littleflame, and all at once, as though a clear signal had been given, they grabbed their possessions, tied up their bundles, shoving in babies, cooking pots, spoons, shoes, garlic and everything, and before the first streaks of dawn had appeared in the sky, they were off—'Ai! Ai! Ai! . . .Ai! Ai! Ai!—. . .'—thump, thump, thump, hurry, hurry, hurry, as though the devil was after them and escape was the only thing that mattered. And there in the middle of the deserted encampment lay poor Littleflame fast asleep, lonely and lost, and a very long way from her home.

When she awoke she looked about disconsolately, but she had hardly expected anything else, not a woman, not a dog, not a goat, not a snake-catcher nor a child.

'If they've left any more babies behind this time, they're not going to get them back!' she said to herself firmly.

Just then two small clouds of dust appeared on the horizon and rushed madly towards her. It was Nannilinka and Kiddilinka approaching in a series of wild leaps like two bouncing balls.

'Good-bye! good-bye! my darling! Keep your heart up! Summer's coming! See you next year!' They were gone, leaping hysterically into the distance.

'Well, anyway, *they* said good-bye,' thought Littleflame, gazing rather sadly after them. 'But why, why, why are they all in such a hurry and can't stop still for even one day?' But it was no good puzzling herself over these things. She had at any rate returned that Intelligent Edible Frog to his ungrateful mother and now she had to find a way of getting herself home again. She doubted whether those proud camels would help her to cross the desert again and anyway they were nowhere to be seen. She thought of the city which she had seen in the mirage and wondered if she could find help there. As the morning mists dissolved she saw its domes and towers appear and started to walk towards it. But soon she found herself on the bank of a wide grey river which flowed between her and the buildings. It was too deep and swift to cross, so she sat down disconsolately on the edge and dabbled her feet and drank a little of the brackish muddy water. The sun was getting hotter and hotter and there was hardly any shade. She curled up behind a rock, drawing herself in as the patch of shade grew smaller and smaller, and fell into a disturbed and unhappy doze.

## On Picking up a Baby

While she was lying under the rock a rowing boat crossed the river and grounded on the bank near her. There were three men in the boat, two dressed in a kind of military uniform with enormous gold epaulettes and brass buttons and belts hung with swords and pistols. The third man had a shabby coat and a black hat and carried a large ledger under his arm. He was the most important of the three and ordered the soldiers about, and every time he ordered them, they saluted and clicked their heels together and said something that sounded like 'Yes sir! No sir! Three bags full sir!' but actually it was not that at all because they spoke a strange language which Littleflame could not understand. She had woken with her head throbbing and her body aching, and she did not know whether it was part of a dream or something that was really happening. The man in the black hat waved his ledger and spluttered angrily at her in a staccato speech which sounded like little guns going off. She could not understand a word and just rubbed her eyes and stared. He tried another language but she shook her head and stared again. He became threatening and the soldiers drew their swords.

'For what evil purpose do you creep like a snake into the heart of the beloved homeland?' he shouted in her own tongue.

'Don't be so cross,' answered Littleflame sleepily. 'I'm not doing any harm.'

'Harm! you crocodile's egg! For what purpose do you come here crawling and sneaking, you spawn of a treacherous jackal? And by what means did you arrive?'

'I came on a camel to take a baby back to his mother.'

'Liar! Cockatrice! Scorpion! Rattlesnake! Where are the camels? Where is the baby? Where is the mother?' He threw his arms wide, gesticulating at the empty desert, and Littleflame had to agree inside herself that her story did not sound convincing.

## On Picking up a Baby

'Answer!' shouted the man, working himself into a fury, and then when she would say no more, he turned to the soldiers and bellowed: 'Arrest her! Put her in chains! Female spy! Vulture! gnawing the vitals of the beloved homeland!'

The soldiers seized Littleflame and clapped handcuffs on to her wrists and dragged her down to the boat. The black-hatted man followed, shouting instructions and stumbling over the stones. As soon as they were all in the boat, the two soldiers started to row like mad, struggling to keep the oars from getting mixed up with their swords, and the black-hatted man opened the ledger and started to write with an enormous red pencil, cursing the soldiers when the boat plunged and pitched under their efforts.

When they reached the other side of the river, the soldiers rowed the boat under a stone archway and a great port-cullis dropped with a splash behind them. They pulled Littleflame roughly out of the boat and dragged her up a flight of stone steps.

'To the dungeons with her!' shouted the angry man, so they marched her on down a dark passage through several locked and massive doors, up and down more stairs, and finally pushed her without ceremony into a small, dark, stone room. She heard the key turn in the lock and then footsteps clank away into the distance.

At any rate the dungeon was beautifully cool and it was a relief to be out of the glare and the heat. Littleflame sat for a while where they had pushed her, listening for footsteps, expecting that someone would come and undo the hand-cuffs and bring her food and drink. But nobody came, so she grew angry and beat with her fists on the door and shouted. Her hands grew sore and her voice hoarse but still nobody came.

There was a little barred window far up above her head

and she thought that, if her hands were free, she might find some way of reaching it, so she knelt down and started to scrape one link of the handcuffs methodically against a stone. She felt sure that anything made in such a stupid country where innocent people were thrown into prison for nothing would be rotten, and she was quite right. The metal was flawed and soft; she soon began to make an impression on it, and before long she had filed through one link and could separate her hands, although the two halves of the handcuffs were still clinging to her wrists. But having made a start, she was encouraged to go on and soon one wrist was free and then the other. She pitched the useless handcuffs into a corner and, feeling much more hopeful, turned round to find some way of reaching the window. To her great surprise an old man was sitting cross-legged on the floor just behind her. He seemed to be deep in thought and hardly conscious of her presence, his hands were folded and his eyes cast down. He looked so ancient and so holy and so kind that she was not at all frightened, only surprised at seeing him sitting there so calmly, as though he had been there all the time.

'Who are you?' she asked in an awed voice.

'Ah! If only I knew!' he sighed deeply and looked up at her.

'But surely you know who you are? I know who I am, but I don't know why they have put me in prison. Why did they put you in prison?'

'They didn't put me in prison. I came myself. It is cool and quiet here and there are no visitors. I go and come as I like.'

'Can you get in and out of the prison then?' Littleflame's hopes began to rise.

'Oh, yes,' he said. 'That is easy.'

'Oh, please, sir, oh, please then, can you show me the

way out? I don't know why they put me here; I haven't
done anything wicked and all I want is to go home. Oh,
please! Can you help?'

The old man looked at her for a long time without
speaking. Then he sighed and motioned to her to sit down
beside him.

'I can help you to get out,' he said, 'but it isn't as easy for
you as it is for me. You see, I can move around in Time and
when I want to get out of the prison or get back into it, I
just go back to a time when the prison wasn't here, or
forward to a time when the prison will have disappeared,
and then, of course, I can walk about as I please, through
the gates, through the walls, down through the ceiling,
anyhow, anywhere. Just now I like being here. It is cool and
quiet and there are no visitors. Everybody forgets you. I
have a problem to solve. When I have solved it, I shall go.'

Littleflame sat silent, pondering what the old man had
said. It did not seem to help her own difficulties very much,
she felt quite bound to the present and terribly hungry as
well.

'Please, sir,' she said very politely after a while, 'I don't
think I really understand very much of what you say, but
please, sir, could you tell me your name?' She wanted to
bring the conversation back to something with which she
felt more familiar.

'People call me Cottonshirt,' he said. 'Eat, child, you
must be hungry.'

To her surprise, Littleflame saw a steaming bowl of rice
and lentils on the floor in front of her and a pitcher of clear
water.

'Is that your supper?' she asked.

'It is yours,' he answered simply.

She needed no more encouragement but cleared the bowl
and the pitcher straight away. Cottonshirt unwound the

shawl that he was wearing about his shoulders and spread it on the floor.

'Sleep,' he said, pointing to it, and although Littleflame wanted to ask more questions and make plans for her escape she remembered what he had said about visitors and quiet. She felt that he did not want to talk any more, so she lay down as she was told and soon fell into the deepest of deep sleeps.

When she awoke she looked about her and saw Cotton-shirt floating half-way up to the ceiling. She found this most astonishing. He was sitting cross-legged on nothing, looking very thoughtful, and Littleflame felt it better not to disturb him. She lay and watched him while he sank slowly to within an inch or two of the floor, where he stayed.

'Eat,' he said for the second time and she found a full bowl and pitcher in front of her. At the sight of the food she realized she was ravenous, but before she started to eat she asked in a puzzled voice:

'Please, sir, can you tell me, am I eating yesterday's dinner to-morrow or to-morrow's dinner today?'

Cottonshirt smiled. 'It is enough that you are hungry and have food to eat,' he answered. 'Three months is a long time to go without food. Eat, and then we will go.'

Littleflame finished the food and water, feeling too puzzled to ask any more questions. Three months certainly was a long time to go without food, but surely she had not been asleep all that time? She looked at Cottonshirt with awe. He was still floating a little way above the ground.

'Now,' he said, 'if you are ready, we will go.'

He stood up and walked towards the door, and before she had realized what was happening he was partly through the nailed and studded wood and one-half of him had disappeared while the other half was disappearing. Then he had gone altogether and she heard the key outside turn in the lock, the door creaked open and there he was standing on the other side smiling at her.

'Come,' he said. 'This is the easiest way to get you out. The gaolers are so lazy here they think everybody is dead and they leave the keys in the locks.'

The awe that Littleflame had felt in seeing him floating in the air was nothing to the awe she felt now that she had seen him flow through the door.

'Oh, sir!' she whispered in a very small voice, 'you are very kind to help me and I wish I could thank you better. But can you help me to understand—I mean—*when* is it? Is it now or before or after and how long?'

He smiled again at her bewilderment. 'You just spent the summer here,' he said. 'It was too hot to go at once; besides, the wild geese don't come until the autumn.'

All that she could answer was: 'Oh!' and, although a thousand questions came into her head, she followed him silently through the long stone passages and up and down the stone stairways, and at each door that they passed, Cottonshirt paused to unlock it and let out the prisoners, who came after them in a shambling silent crowd, and every time they came to a door across the passage-way, Cottonshirt flowed through it and unlocked it from the other side. No one spoke and it was as if the whole strange company was passing through a dream.

Soon they came out on the steps by the river. A sentry was marching up and down, clanking his sword and munching a huge sandwich and mumbling orders to some men unloading stores from boats. The portcullis was up and more boats were coming in from the river, all loaded with boxes marked 'Ham' or 'Kippers' or 'Flour' or 'Eggs' or 'Fish Jam'. Littleflame's heart sank when she saw all the men, and she thought that all hope of escape was gone. The sentry was gobbling great bites from his sandwich and his mouth was crammed full. Cottonshirt walked up to him and took a paper from under his shawl.

'Orders for release of prisoners,' he said authoritatively.

The sentry jumped to attention, dropped his sandwich and took the paper. On it was written 'Release at once and transfer to other containers'. It had come off one of the boxes marked 'Crab'. He shouted something incoherent from his mouth still full of sandwich, and the men unloading the stores came running up the steps and the prisoners ran past them down the steps and piled into the loaded boats and pushed off. The dazed sentry, realizing his mistake and trying to save his sandwich from being trodden on, was knocked into the water, but not before he had shouted, 'Down with the portcullis!' Cottonshirt and Littleflame were in the last boat and the current seized them as they reached open water. There was a confused shouting and cursing behind them and with a great splash the portcullis fell, shutting in the guards and shutting out the prisoners.

It was a motley fleet that fanned out across the river, but every boat was loaded with stores, so no one would lack supplies. Very soon the stream had spread them far and wide and most of the boats were just black dots disappearing into the distance. It was growing dark and there was a confusion of shouts and bugle calls from the town and Littleflame could see hundreds of people hurrying about carrying flares. She shivered apprehensively in the cold air.

'Do you think they will try and catch everybody again?' she asked.

'It would be difficult,' Cottonshirt answered gravely. 'You see, I have let everybody out, past and future prisoners as well. There would be difficulty with some of those.' He smiled gently at her. 'Now, my child, there is only your journey home.'

They grounded on a sandbank and climbed out and

# On Picking up a Baby

Cottonshirt pushed the boat with its cargo back into the stream. Littleflame had seen too many unusual things to doubt that this was the right thing to do and she sat down beside Cottonshirt on the damp sand. Boats with torches were crossing the river and passing quite close to them, but nobody seemed to see them. The boats reached the far shore and there was much shouting and cursing and the torches moved up and down until one by one they started to go out, and the soldiers and townspeople struggled back again across the river in the dark, swearing and blaming each other as they went.

'What's going to happen now?' asked Littleflame, as they had been sitting there for a long time. The night was cold and she could see no way of getting off the sandbank.

'Our friends the geese are coming to take you home,' answered Cottonshirt. 'Listen and you will hear them in a little while.'

'Am I really going to fly home on a goose?' exclaimed Littleflame. 'What a lot of creatures will have carried me on this journey! Whatever would the others say!'

Just then there was a faint whistling in the dark overhead and a rushing of pinions drawing closer as the geese landed by them one by one on the sand. She could see their heads and necks silhouetted dimly against the stars.

'Am I really going now? Are you coming too? Oh, please let me see you again, there are so many things I want to know. . . .'

Before she had finished speaking and before there was any answer from Cottonshirt she was off. She nestled into the warm down on the goose's back while the pale sandbank and Cottonshirt's ghostly form disappeared below and the stars brightened in the clearer air as they rose. Her first feeling was one of tremendous excitement at the thought of flying home, her second was one of regret that without realizing it she had left Cottonshirt with none of her burning questions answered and no means of ever finding him again. Then the swift movement of flight turned her thoughts to the long laborious journey which she had made on the invisible earth now below her, the swaying camels, the galloping horses, the trotting donkeys, her own sore feet, Tadpole, Nannilinka, the Snake Gypsies and her boat, and how it had all started by just playing a game about the Tungi People. With little lamps the adventure had begun and with little lamps it was going to end, because far underneath her she saw her own village, and every house was outlined with sparks of light, and she remembered with a pang that summer had gone and that autumn had come and already the night had been reached when all the lost spirits were called home and lamps put out to guide them.

'Am I a lost spirit?' she asked and pinched herself to find out.

The whistling pinions of the goose changed tone. They were slowing down and losing height, the great bird's body tilted and its neck reared up as it came in to land. They were down and she threw her arms round its neck and kissed it on the beak.

'Oh, thank you, thank you! And good-bye, and please tell Cottonshirt I love him and I want to see him again!'

The goose was gone and she heard his ghostly wings as he rose, and saw a patch of stars blotted out for a moment as she stood in the dark, not knowing whether she was glad or sorry. Then she turned towards the little lamp-lit houses on the short stretch of this long journey which still lay between her and her home.

# The House that had learned
# to keep still

For a long time after Littleflame had left him, Tob sat playing with his measuring rod, his shadows and his triangles. The long morning shadow thrown by the rod when he set it upright in the sand was growing shorter and soon it was no longer than the rod itself. Here surely was the magic moment when the sun was giving the answer clearly without any of those puzzling problems it set when the shadow was too short or too long. Tob clasped his head in his paws and held his breath. At last he knew it! He was a discoverer! At that moment, that exact and absolute moment, all shadows fitted, were exactly the length of the things they shadowed—the rod's shadow, his own shadow, the shadows of the trees, even the shadow of the mountains thrown across the valleys (but you would have to gallop very fast to measure them before they changed). He sat hugging himself ecstatically; then, seizing his measuring rod, he scampered off through the trees, his mind brimming with all the wonderful things he was going to do.

He would measure towers and palaces for kings, he would tell wise men how high their mountains were, he would find the heights of the tallest trees in the forests. And everybody would wonder how he did it with nothing but a little notched stick to help him. He galloped on joyfully until a small uncomfortable thought crept into his mind. Supposing nobody wanted to know the height of his towers or his mountains or his trees? His pace slackened to a subdued walk and then the clouds came down on the forest and there were no more shadows and that put an end to measuring and to most of his thoughts of fame. Soon mist was everywhere, heavy drops hung upon the pine needles, the path under his feet was sodden and soft, there was no light, no shade, only a subdued melancholy flatness as though the forest had been stitched upon tapestry. He padded along thoughtfully, a small two-dimensional animal in a silent two-dimensional world.

' 'Twere main dafty!' he mused, imagining that he had arrived at a palace where the one thing the king really wanted was to know how high his chimneys were and then it had started to rain and the weather had not cleared up for days and days. Tob decided there were better ways of becoming famous than by measuring the chimneys of kings. He decided to go uphill and see what he could find.

The hillside was covered with pine needles and almost as slippery as ice, but scrambling up with the help of all his claws he reached a ridge along which was a path which widened into a well-marked track. Suddenly he was out of the clouds and in the sun again, or rather his head was in the sun although the rest of him was still in cloud. This seemed very strange to Tob and he stopped here to experiment, sunning his head above the cloud, then standing on his head and sticking his feet out into the sun and wiggling his toes in the warmth. He tried to catch pieces of cloud in his paws and put them on his head like a hat, he tried biting up mouthfuls and swallowing them, but they were so slippery and unsatisfying that he could not really tell whether he had got them or not. He thought he would make up a poem about this or perhaps a riddle and puzzle his family with it when he got home.

Above the cloud the path climbed on in a series of zigzags. He kept crossing and re-crossing a little stream, sometimes on stepping stones, sometimes on logs and sometimes just by jumping. He stopped again to find out how fast the water ran by throwing sticks into the stream and racing down with them over waterfalls and along the shallows where the stream flowed slowly over yellow pebbles. But as he was trying to go uphill and the stream was succeeding in coming downhill, he found that this game was just taking him back from where he had come. So he left his sticks to float down into the valley while he himself climbed back again along the zigzags.

After a while he came upon a stone bridge and on the bridge, swinging his legs above the water, sat a small old man cracking walnuts. He smiled at Tob and his face wrinkled up like one of his walnuts. He patted the stone beside him and signed to Tob to sit down. Then he went on cracking nuts and the two of them shared the kernels together.

They spoke not a word, but Tob soon saw that the old man was playing a game with himself. He put two walnuts together in his hands, then squeezed until one walnut cracked the other. The cracked walnut was eaten while the whole walnut was given another walnut to crack and if one nut won nine victories it was put on one side carefully. After a while there was quite a pile of 'niners' and between them

Tob and the old man had eaten a prodigious number of nuts. Tob tried his hand at the game but he squashed both walnuts so flat that there was no victor and no vanquished and no possibility of unmixing the nut from the shell.

' 'Tis Tob as can't never crack nuts proper but 'tis Tob as kin sing,' he said when he felt he could eat no more.

The old man nodded vigorously and went on eating his nuts. This is the song that Tob sang:

> 'When you done eat it for your dinner
>   You fills up full but gets much thinner,
>   When you done use it for a bed
>   You falls down flat and breaks your head,
>   When you done stick it in your hair
>   You sticks it hard but 'tisn't there.
>   When you done name its name out loud
>   It's never nothing but a . . .'

'Cloud!' shouted the old man at the top of his voice. He jumped up and started tossing all his 'niners' in the air, keeping them all going at once like a juggler, flicking them behind his back, under his knees, off his elbows, all at such a pace that Tob began to feel quite dizzy watching. He stared in delighted astonishment and wished he had that skill to use at home with the tossers.

'Apples and pears!' he shouted delightedly, and the old man bowed and sat down again beside him. So far Tob had heard him utter only one word and he began to wonder whether he was much good at talking, but he thought he would try him with one question.

'Thank'ee, mister,' he began politely. 'This here road do be main twisty an' slopey. Who done live up yon?'

He pointed up the hill to where the zigzag road disappeared over the crest. At once the expression changed on the old man's face. He looked shocked and frightened and started to gather up his 'niners' and stow them carefully in his pockets. Then he stood up and looked cautiously all round, leaned down towards Tob and shook his forefinger at him severely.

'Dorn't'ee never go a seekin' after them wipsy people what lives up yon,' he said in a hoarse whisper. 'They ain't properly in nature. You leave them be or WHANG! they'll fix you flatter nor any nut!' And to emphasize his point, he took out one of the 'niners', put it in his left hand, then brought his right hand down on it like a hammer and held out the flattened remains to Tob upon his palm.

'Flatter nor thatter!' he said grimly, and turning his back he walked off across the hillside.

Tob watched him go, then considered what he should do. He looked up the zigzag road, which was still in bright sunlight and seemed as safe as most sunlit roads on a peaceful afternoon. He could see no harm in going to the top, especially if he turned round and came straight down again as soon as he had seen what was on the other side. It looked inviting, so he set off, intending to be cautious and wondering if there was any substance in the old man's warning. The road was steep and he counted the breaths it took to a zig and then the breaths it took to a zag and played off the zigs against the zags until he had quite forgotten his resolutions and arrived at the top, where the road levelled off between an avenue of pines and then ran out into an open glade. A wind blew through the trees, making a delicious sighing. There was a warm winy smell and he found he was stepping on wild strawberries and crushing them under his feet. He started to pull them up in great handfuls, leaves and all, and stuffed them into his mouth, drinking and eating at the same time while the warm juice ran down his fur. Then he lay on his back and rolled on the strawberries until he was covered with squashed fruit and sticky all over. Then he sat down to clean it all off with his paws and tongue. He did this five times until he was absolutely full of strawberry inside and as clean as a whistle outside. Then he sat up and looked about him.

Just across the glade from where he was sitting he was surprised to see a little house under a tree. He had not noticed it before, but perhaps that was because he was so busy with the strawberries. It was quite a small house, built of logs and thatched with straw. It had two windows and a door and the windows had carved shutters which made them look like eyes and the handle of the door was in the middle, which made it look like a nose. There were two wobbly chimneys which looked like ears, and it was all balanced on four crooked posts which looked like bony little legs. But the oddest thing about the house was that it seemed to be in a high wind. Smoke was blowing out horizontally from the chimneys and a piece of branch caught in the thatch was lashing to and fro in a furious gale. But round about Tob the trees were now quite still and there was not breeze enough to stir the grass.

This was so strange that Tob sat staring at the house while the house stared back at him and, after they had been staring for some time, Tob thought he saw one of the window shutters close and open again very slowly, almost as though the house had winked. The hairs rose in a bristly ridge along his back and he started to sidle slowly round the house, keeping his distance but examining first the sides and then the back, where there were no windows but another very small door which looked a little like a tail. Tob watched the house suspiciously for some time but there was no further sign of life, no winks, no movement except what was caused by its own peculiar private wind snatching the smoke from its chimneys.

Still unable to feel it was quite an ordinary house he turned his back and walked away, and when he had walked some distance he turned round suddenly and faced the house. There it was under its tree, just a house and no more. Tob thought he must either be very stupid or perhaps intoxicated by the strawberries; he had come upon another patch of delicious fruit and started to stuff himself again. When he could not eat another berry he sat up to look for the house again. It was not there. There was the tree but no house.

He stood on his hind legs and peered all round the glade and there to his relief was the house, still under a tree, but which tree? He must have made a mistake and lost his sense of direction. He cuffed his ears several times smartly, shook himself severely and started to walk towards the house. Dusk was falling, it was too late to go home and he must find somewhere to spend the night. He went firmly up to the front door and knocked. There was no answer, so he pushed the door open and walked in, and the wind slammed the door to behind him.

Inside, the house was warm and inviting. There were two fireplaces and two fires were burning brightly, one in each hearth. In one corner was a pile of deliciously scented branches laid out as a bed, and if it had not been for the rattle made by the wind, Tob could not have imagined a nicer place to spend the night. He threw himself down on the springy sweet-smelling branches and soon he was snoring away happily, cracking walnuts and zigzagging up mountain paths in his dreams. He woke once during the night. The fires were still burning and sending shadows dancing up and down the walls, but the wind had dropped and everything seemed quiet. He fell asleep again.

When Tob had entered the house in the evening he had looked carefully at the tree under which it stood and at the grass with which it was surrounded. The tree was a pine with a twisted trunk and there were small blue flowers scattered among the grass. When he opened the door in the morning he was shocked to find that there was almost nothing in front of the house at all, only a few precarious thorn bushes, then a drop into a deep empty valley. He stepped gingerly out of doors with his back hairs tingling and sidled to safety along the cliff edge. He walked a few hundred paces with his head glued anxiously over his shoulder, ready to bolt at any moment. He put a solid hillock between himself and the house and then settled down to an uneasy breakfast of strawberries. He became engrossed in his meal, burying his nose in the leaves and gobbling greedily. When he looked up his heart gave a great thump. There was the house standing just under the hillock with the path that he had trodden carefully placed so that it looked as though it had always been the path to the front door.

At first Tob was too frightened to move. He remained petrified with the half-eaten strawberries in his mouth. Nothing happened and the house looked so ordinary that he began to relax, then gathering all the courage he could muster he gave a tremendous woof! and turned and galloped off as fast as he could. When he had put a good distance between himself and the house, he turned round and looked cautiously. The house seemed to be in the same place; he could see the roof and the chimneys clearly although the rest was hidden by bushes. Feeling relieved, he started to creep away through the undergrowth, hoping to find his way back on to the path which would lead him down the zigzags and back again to his home. But suddenly he remembered his measuring rod! He had carried it carefully all the previous day and had stood it against the wall beside his bed before he had gone to sleep. Now it was gone and he tried desperately to remember whether he had picked it up when he had left the house or whether it was still indoors. He was torn between fear of the house and grief at losing the rod. He could not bear the idea of never seeing it again, it had taken hours of patient work to smooth and mark and had been the companion to one of the proudest moments of his life.

He started to slink back the way he had come, using the greatest caution, wriggling his way along the ground, hardly daring to lift his head above the grasses, and stopping to snuff and peer at every suspicious smell or sound. He reached the hillock and wormed his way to the top and lifted himself inch by inch until he was just high enough to see over the other side.

There was nothing there at all, not a window, not a roof, not a chimney, not a door, just a little empty patch of grass waving in the breeze. But right beside him on the crest of the hillock, standing upright in the ground, was the precious measuring rod and fixed on to the top was a piece of thin bark paper and on the paper was a picture drawn in pinkish ink.

He looked at the picture and turned it over and smelled it. The ink was sticky and he licked it; it tasted like strawberry juice. He did not like to stay too long on this uncanny piece of ground so he gathered up the picture and his measuring rod and crept away to a thick patch of trees where he could watch but stay hidden himself. There he lay on his stomach and studied the drawing carefully.

It seemed to be a kind of map. There was the sun on one side throwing out its rays, there was a zigzag line going up the middle like the road on which he had travelled. And, of course, that is just what the line was meant to be because there were the sun's rays casting shadows from his measuring rod and the woolly upper surface of the cloud, and his own feet sticking out into the sunlight. Then he could see the stream and the bridge and nine walnuts and a giant strawberry plant above. Then the pine tree and the little house with the smoke blowing from its chimneys and then the hillock with the measuring rod standing upright on it

with the picture fixed to the top. So far that had all happened, but now came the really interesting bit because it must show what was going to happen. The zigzag road went farther up, and at the top were two strange signs like question marks, and above everything else—and this made Tob's eyes glitter—was a most gorgeous crown studded with jewels and throwing out rays of strawberry-coloured light. Whatever could this mean? Was Tob going to be made a king? Or was some wonderful royal personage waiting for him at the top of those zigzags and between those two question marks?

He threw caution to the winds. Holding the map in front of him as a guide he started to march boldly away in the direction in which he guessed the further zigzags should be. He soon found that he was right; the road twisted sharply away again backwards and forwards up the hill. He played no games of zigs against zags but stopped at each bend and peered carefully upwards before starting on the next. He got hot and thirsty and longed for some strawberries, but here it was stony and no plants were growing. He pushed on upwards, brimming with curiosity and thinking all the time of that crown.

Presently he passed through an iron gate which was swinging open on rusty hinges and then suddenly he saw the question marks. He stopped dead in the middle of the road with his heart in his mouth. He would have bolted, but it was too late, he knew that he had been seen. He stood there for a minute, gathering his wits, then marched straight on boldly, looking as unconcerned as he could, just as though he had every right to be where he was now sure that he should not be.

And what do you suppose those question marks were?

They were the long, black, curly tails of two immense black cats who were standing one on each side of the road, just beyond the gate, with their tails curled up behind them like great interrogation marks, and between their tails was slung a notice board which read:—

*TO THE CONTEST*
*1st Prize* — A PRINCESS
*2nd Prize* — A FEAST
ALL FAILED CONTESTANTS MUST JOIN THE 2ND
and
be feasted on.
LISTS CLOSE AT ELEVEN
SHARP

If you had been there to read this notice you would have been wise enough to turn round and go straight home in spite of the cats. But Tob had never learned to read, so he could not tell what the notice board said, and he walked on firmly between the two rather terrible cats under the ominous notice board and right into the middle of a very extraordinary adventure.

The road went on straight and flat and up the centre marched Tob, shouldering his measuring rod like a gun and looking much braver than he felt. He knew that the cats had turned round to look at him because he could feel their hard green eyes boring into his back. He wanted to bolt but he made himself walk steadily on without looking behind until he was sure he was out of sight. Then he stopped and peered carefully behind and in front and on each side of him.

'I did oughter see that there crown afore long,' he muttered to himself and took another look at the map. The crown was certainly the next thing that he should come to, and he thought he could hear a muffled noise ahead which he felt must have something to do with it. He went on until the road came to an abrupt stop at the edge of a steep drop and a wide stone stairway led down into an amphitheatre surrounded by tiers of seats. The seats were filled with curious-looking goblins and the noise was made by their voices calling hoarsely to each other across the arena. Tob peered over the edge and decided that it would be better to remain unseen. The goblins certainly looked sinister and strange and unlike anything he had seen before. They had elongated faces and their eyes were set sideways so that the corners were up and down instead of horizontal. This gave them a vicious melancholy appearance accentuated by small drooping mouths with protruding teeth somewhere where their chins should have been. They had ears like pigs' ears, and small clawed and webbed hands with which they clung on to the ruinous seats and scrabbled up and down between the tiers. The whole place had a broken-down neglected look and piles of rubbish were lying about, old chair legs, gnawed bones and cabbage stumps and stale pieces of paper floating from one place to another.

There was no crown anywhere to be seen, only this slummy uncared-for place with its grubby unpleasing people, and Tob found this most disappointing. He was about to creep away when there was a sudden uproar among the goblins, who started to chant a rhythmic cry: 'Omo! Daz! Omo! Daz!' and bang their heads with their hands, which caused a dull thundering rattle to circle round the arena. Some frantic late-comers scuttled by Tob, so anxious to reach their places that they quite overlooked him. There was nowhere to hide, but he lay as flat as he could and peered over the edge to see what was going on.

All at once there was a great commotion in one corner, some goblins started to beat drums and some to toot trumpets, and out stepped a very grand tall goblin dressed in yellow and purple, and behind him a smaller but even more important goblin dressed in purple and pink. And the second goblin had something shining and winking and glittering on her head.

'Squeeze my paws if that isn't never that there crown what's in the picture!' Tob shouted out loud, but there was enough noise down below to drown his voice. He was terribly excited. He clasped his paws and watched the two royal goblins cross the arena to the frenzied shrieks of the crowd. 'Omo! Daz! Omo! Daz!' they roared till the royal ones reached a raised dais and the yellow and purple king held up his hand for silence. There was an immediate hush and the king began to make a speech, but Tob could only hear a few words because his voice was muffled and hoarse and the dais was immediately below where Tob lay, so that the king was facing away from him.

'Citizens . . . fellow goblins . . . annual contest . . . prize which has never been won . . . delicious feast . . . wider horizons . . . well-loved incomparable princess . . .' Tob hardly listened, but his eyes were riveted on the crown with its enormous pink and white jewels, and on the princess who was under the crown in her pink and purple gown studded with winking shining ornaments. He could not see her face but he was convinced she must be beautiful, forlorn, misunderstood and greatly in need of rescuing. He stuffed both front paws into his mouth to keep himself from shouting out in his excitement.

The king had finished his speech and had sat down on his throne with the princess beside him. There was a roar of applause and a dozen white-aproned goblins ran into the arena carrying an enormous pole. They laid it on the ground and made deep obeisance towards the throne. They then started to raise the pole into an upright position, staying it with long ropes stretched out towards the circumference of the arena. When all the ropes were fixed and the pole in position a goblin with a trumpet stepped out into the middle, blew a blast and announced:

'First item in the contest! Measuring the flagpole! All contestants stand forth!'

Tob's eyes almost popped out of his head with astonishment. Measuring! Measuring! Measuring! He clutched his little rod and looked at the sun. It was shining bright and clear, beautifully defined dark shadows were being thrown on the ground. Down below a little man clutching a coil of rope was starting to shin up the pole. He looked like a small grey monkey and for the first few feet he got on splendidly and the crowd roared. He got higher and higher and slower and slower and the crowd hissed and jeered and shouted.

He was nearly at the top, he reached up and started to uncoil his rope and fix it to the top, he slipped and there was a yell of wicked laughter, he struggled upwards again, clung for an agonizing second while the rope blew out on the wind and he looked like a spider starting to spin her web, when all at once to the accompaniment of a revolting shout of mockery he was slithering down hopelessly and meeting the ground with a sickening thump, his rope lying in tangles and knots about him.

'Stew him! Mince him! Hash him! Baste him!' screamed the crowd while the white-aproned goblins hurried him off on a stretcher.

Tob should have been warned, but he was not. He watched another wretched contestant go through the same performance and a third who had thought of the bright idea of getting most of the way up by a ladder, but they all ended up in battered heaps on the ground, to be carried off by the officials to the ravenous cheers of the crowd. Tob's heart was fluttering, he was bouncing up and down muttering furiously to himself.

''Tis them poor dafty fools as won't never do it! 'Tis I kin do it! 'Tis I kin do it! 'Tis Tob kin do it!'

At last he could bear it no longer and bursting from his watching place he took the steps of the stone stairway in a series of reckless leaps and hurled himself into the middle of the arena, his mind closed to everything except just that one over-riding problem of how to measure the pole.

'Let I!' he commanded the astonished officials. 'Do'ee all stand back! 'Tis Tob'll say how tall she be!'

He had taken command of the situation. The goblin officials, looking rather dazed, withdrew to the sides. With still a little sense left in his head Tob remembered the king, made a deep bow in the direction of the dais and then set to work. He was lucky. He set up his rod erect in the ground, marked its shadow and measured it. To his delight the rod and the shadow were the same length. Here was his magic moment again and he walked confidently to the base of the pole, placed the rod on its shadow and measured it step by step along its length, counting carefully as he went. When he reached the end of the shadow, which was near the edge of the arena—and he could hear the goblins above him breathing heavily—he stood up and said in a loud triumphant voice:

'A hunderd fifty two an' a half bears' feet she be an' our Mam did say as 'tis the same as what other folks do measure by, so a hunderd fifty two an' a half feet she be!'

There was the silence of complete amazement in the goblin crowd, followed by a murmur growing to a roar, and furious voices could be distinguished:—

'Climb it! Miserable cheat!'

'Slice him! Spoil-sport!'

'Skin him!'

'Fry him!'

'Hash him!'

'Stick him in aspic!'

'Where's our bread and circuses?'

Frenzied officials raced round lashing at the crowd with whips to keep them in order. The king seized a megaphone and bellowed in a terrible voice:

'Silence! Or I'll curry you all and throw you to the Cats! Impudent animal with four paws—come here!'

Suddenly becoming aware of the furious audience, Tob's senses started to return. He wondered whatever had made him jump into that arena of death and pit himself against such an array of demons with only his home-made measuring rod and his overweening conceit between himself and certain obliteration. He blinked miserably, and the pale spectacle rings around his eyes made him look very perplexed and forsaken.

'Come here!' The king's voice bellowed out again through the megaphone and then all that could be heard was the scrunch of the pebbles under Tob's paws as he approached gingerly across the arena. He reached a place a few yards in front of the king and stopped. He bowed very low, then raised his eyes cautiously and caught sight of the princess's face under the glittering crown. She was smiling at him with a blank meaningless smile, the sort of smile that would have been taught at a goblin's deportment school. Tob was shocked and quickly lowered his eyes again. Never before had he seen such an ugly face or conjured one up in a nightmare. What a price for the crown! He closed his eyes and sat stock still like a stone waiting to be engulfed by a wave, and prayed silently inside his head.

'Please, I won't never be hump-headed no more. Please, I won't never go where I didn't oughter go. I isn't nothin' but a scraffetty small stoopidest bear that don't know nothin' an' won't never know nothin'. Please, I don't never want to be cooked nor hashed nor curried nor nothin'. An' PLEASE I don't never want no prizes!'

He kept his eyes shut and still nothing happened, so he added as a rider to his prayer in the smallest inside voice he could conjure: 'Just the same they's a lot o' foolish know-nouts what I could learn a lot if they'd a mind to!' He fluttered his eyes and peeped out.

The king looked truly awful. He was muttering with one of the officials and his face was all swollen and red with anger. The princess was still smiling, but she did not seem able to do anything else and her empty grin was quite terrifying.

'Approach nearer!' commanded the king, and Tob took another two steps forward and made such a very low bow that his head touched the ground and he kept it there cautiously until the king spoke again.

'Was your name entered in the lists?' demanded the king in an awful voice.

Tob, who thought that this was some kind of an accusation, shook his head and answered, 'I never!' then added as a tactful afterthought, 'I didn't never your reverence.'

'There you are!' shouted the king. 'You've broken the rules and should be minced. But you've got the answer right so you've got to have the prize too!'

Tob shook his head and looked more miserable than ever.

'A hundred and fifty-two and a half feet, you said, and a hundred and fifty-two and a half feet it is, and how you found it out by just walking along the ground with four paws and a stick is more than I can say! Impudence! Plain impudence! You've spoilt the game and we'll have to get a new pole! Disrespect and impudence!' The king kept bellowing through the megaphone and his voice was deafening.

'I knowed it by this here stick,' said Tob sullenly and enigmatically, and stuffed his paws into his ears.

The king seemed almost too angry to speak and pulled one of the officials roughly towards him and started to growl angrily into his ear. They consulted for a minute, then an evil smile crept over the king's face.

'Ha! ha!' he croaked in a guttural voice. 'All right! All right! You're disqualified so you must be hashed, but you've won, so you get the prize. But this is all very unusual, so first we'll put you through the riddle game. Ha! ha! One answer wrong—*or right*—you'll get the prize, you'll be hashed *and* you'll be curried as well. There's justice for you! Which would you like first?' He reached out and tweaked Tob's ear playfully.

'Which of what?' asked Tob, who had only just taken his paws from his ears.

'The Prize?' leered the King, pushing the smiling princess towards Tob. 'Hashing?' He pulled the princess back and made appropriate chopping motions in the air with his arms. 'Or currying?' He stirred his arms about violently and made snapping and sucking noises with his teeth.

'I'll be hashed,' said Tob decidedly.

'Who told you to choose?' shouted the king angrily. 'Clear the arena! This is my fun, I'm going to have you *all* to myself and REALLY ENJOY you!'

The goblin officials hurried round shooing the goblins out of their seats. They scratched and scrabbled their way out, grumbling angrily at being cheated of their entertainment, and soon there was nobody left except the king, the princess with two attendants, one goblin official in a white apron and Tob. The king slapped his thighs, sucked his teeth and rasped his clawed hands together.

'Now,' he said with a satisfied smile, sinking back comfortably on to his throne. 'Now for the riddles! And remember—if you get one answer wrong—OR RIGHT—— Sit down and think, because it's the last time you'll ever sit or think!'

Tob sat and did his best to think, but whichever way he looked at the situation his fate was not promising and the order in which his sentences were to be carried out did not seem to be of great importance. He peeped again at the princess and decided that hashing would be preferable as a start.

'Number one riddle!' shouted the king through the megaphone, as though they had all been a mile off. 'Attention! TABULAR NEBULA FEET IN HEAD OUT HEAD IN FEET OUT NEBULA TABULAR NOWT!'

'Clouds what's in the valley,' answered Tob promptly and looked round to see who had spoken, because he was certain that he was far too frightened to say anything himself.

'Right!' roared the king and looked so dreadfully red and angry that Tob thought he was going to have a fit.

'Number two riddle!' shouted the king even louder this time. 'Attention! HAMMER JAMMER BANG SWAT YOU'RE FLAT I'M NOT!'

'Walnuts!' This answer seemed so idiotic to Tob he was convinced that somebody else had made it, but it had come out of his own mouth all the same. The king was almost speechless and ground his teeth together like rocks breaking in an earthquake.

'Right again!' he hissed, 'and if you're right next time I'll not only hash and curry you but marinade you in tar and boil your whiskers off! Number three riddle! Attention! YOU THINK I MOVE I KNOW I DON'T YOU THINK YOU'RE STILL I KNOW I AM ALTHOUGH I AM AS STILL AS INK THAT DRAWS THESE QUESTION MARKS IN PINK OR SO YOU THINK!' He leaned forward and fixed Tob with his awful eye, his teeth chattering in anticipation.

'That's done me proper!' thought Tob. It did not seem to matter very much whether the answers he gave were wrong or right, but he felt he would prefer to go to the hashing or whatever was waiting for him with the right answers rather than the wrong ones. He considered for a moment and realized that the answers he had so far made to these idiotic riddles were all something to do with the way in which he had reached this curious place, so he had a good clue to the answer of this one.

' 'Tis that small little house,' he answered and was going to add 'what wouldn't keep still', but the end of his sentence was lost in the final explosion of the king's anger. He had fallen flat on his back with a great clang and the terrified official was gesticulating madly and pushing Tob and the princess with her two attendant goblins towards the steps.

'Quick! Quick! Get out!' he implored. 'No one's ever got them all right before. If he comes round and finds any of you here at all, he'll hash the lot of us. Get out! Get out!'

He hustled them up the broken steps between the seats, and as they reached the top they looked back to see him leaning anxiously over the king and fanning him with his apron. It was no time to hesitate, the remaining problems would have to be sorted out later, and Tob took the princess firmly by her scaly hand and, followed by the two attendant goblins, started to march back along the road on which he had come.

Their progress was slow. The princess was dreadfully over-dressed and her shoes were enormous. The crown kept slipping, and every few yards she stopped to adjust it or hitch up her voluminous shining skirts or pull on a shoe by pushing a grubby claw in the heel. Tob hardly dared to look at her but walked along solemnly holding her scaly hand, and if he released it to allow her to adjust her clothes she would quickly seize his paw again and hold him fast. He felt it would not be difficult to escape from this ponderous personage, but the two young goblins looked both active and formidable. In any case the cats had still to be passed and his unpleasant companions would probably guarantee that he got by them safely, which he might not do by himself.

The young goblins, who had been trotting obediently behind the princess, soon became tired of the slow pace and started to pinch and slap each other spitefully. Their attacks became more and more vicious and noisy until suddenly their mistress, tiring of their quarrels and bad temper, turned round and seized one in each hand, cracked their skulls together with a resounding bang and shoved one in each pocket of her skirt. She was now more immobilized than ever and the goblins hung there dolefully with oily tears trickling down their faces. Tob, who expected them to be either dead or stunned after such treatment, stole a curious glance at the two horrid creatures. One had deep sunken eyes which almost disappeared into their sockets, while his companion's eyes moved restlessly on stalks like a snail's. The princess slapped the sunken-eyed goblin on the side of the head and addressed Tob with a croaky giggle:

'Thrum-eye!' she said.

Then she slapped the stalk-eyed goblin on the side of the head and said: 'Pin-eye!' and giggled again. So Tob at any rate knew their names, although it did not make him like them any better.

The tips of the cats' ears soon came in sight and the princess shook Pin-eye and Thrum-eye out of her pockets, straightened her crown, hitched up her skirt, held up her head and went forward with a rather less slovenly gait. The cats had been washing their faces as all cats do after a heavy meal and Tob wondered nervously what they had been eating. As soon as they saw the princess approaching they sprang up and arched their tails over the road for the company to pass through. Every hair on Tob's back stood out stiffly like a needle and again he felt as though the cats' eyes were boring through him like augers. He looked neither to right nor left, but for once felt grateful for the rasping hand of the princess tightly clutching his paw.

Then it began to rain and soon a more miserable group of creatures could hardly be imagined. Pin-eye and Thrum-eye trotted along whining wretchedly, the tears running from Pin-eye like a leaky tap and oozing from Thrum-eye down his neck and into his clothes. They became so sodden and pitiable Tob wondered whether they might melt and dissolve away altogether, which would have solved the problem of his escape. They seemed to guess his thoughts and clung viciously to his other paw, so that he could not even wipe the water from his face. The princess's shoes filled with water and her heavy skirt clogged her legs. Her pockets appeared to be waterproof and filled with rain which slopped hopelessly to and fro at each step like over-filled buckets. There seemed to be no reason for their wretched progress except to put as much distance as possible between themselves and the angry king.

Presently the princess stopped, put her nose up into the air and set up a heartrending wail.

'I want to go home! I want to go home!' she cried.

'We want to go home! We want to go home!' echoed Pin-eye and Thrum-eye.

'I wish I done been hashed!' muttered Tob gloomily and contemplated his sodden companions until a wave of disgust and anger came over him.

'If you isn't never the miserablist, soppiest, dampest lot o' rotten ole turnips, 'tisn't Tob as says not! Empty your pockets an' step out, you girt sloppy thing! 'Tisn't never no good a-screechin' an' a-shoutin' an' a-creatin' like a lot o' damp ewes! Get you home if you've a mind! 'Tisn't Tob as'll be callin' for you to come back not for all the crowns an' jools in Skamskatka!' He angrily shook his paws free and stood glaring at them as fiercely as he could, very surprised at his own audacity.

The princess was astonished. She leaned down and stared at Tob as though she had never seen him before and a kaleidoscope of changing expressions passed over her face, fury, bewilderment, misery; then it crumpled into a knot of agonized wrinkles and she burst into tears. Tob's heart smote him, but he felt desperate.

'If you was wantin' to get home,' he said sullenly, ''tisn't never that way that you be goin'.'

'I want to go to your home!' cried the princess between her convulsive sobs and her eyelashes fluttered like rags in the wind.

''Twouldn't never do,' answered Tob firmly. ''Tis full up wi' bears.'

'I'll turn them out,' sobbed the princess, recovering a little. 'It'll be just you and me.'

Tob did not answer, because he was wondering anxiously what the effect would be on his mother and father and Cob and Nob and Hob if he arrived home with this awkward princess and her two retainers. The thought made him very uncomfortable, but they could not stay there; dusk was falling and some place to spend the night must be found.

''Tis like we best be gettin' on,' he said, and the princess sidled up to him in her squelchy shoes.

The rain had grown less and they were slowly coming down the first series of zigzags. To get the princess around the sharp corners was a formidable task. She did not seem to have the sense to turn and would only go in the direction in which she was headed. Every time a corner was reached she would plunge straight over the edge of the road unless forcibly faced round by Pin-eye and Thrum-eye with the help of Tob. As darkness fell they reached the first stretch of level ground in an exhausted state and shambled on with very little idea of where to go or what to do. Tob could smell the strawberries but he was too miserable to care. All at once two bright lights shone out in front of them and to Tob's inexpressible relief they found themselves standing outside the mysterious little house.

'Home at last!' croaked the princess and threw her sodden arms around Tob.

''Tis Chooseday an' the bears has choosed to be out,' he said with great presence of mind. 'Do'ee step in, mam.' He opened the door grandly and they all walked in.

The house was warm and inviting and the two fires were burning brightly in the hearths. But it hardly seemed the place for a princess with only a pile of branches to sit on and absolutely nothing else at all. She looked around her with a dull stare, then sank on to the branches with a groan. The jewelled crown rolled off her head and dark water trickled out of her shoes and crept in a slow stream across the floor. Tob picked up the crown and placed it right in the middle of the room because he did not know what else to do, and then he stood and scratched his head. Pin-eye and Thrum-eye brightened up immediately. They shook themselves violently so that the fires hissed and leaped, then stood themselves stiffly one each side of the princess.

'Ho!' she said trying to regain some of her confidence. 'Ho! Bring supper, dry clothes, wine and sweetmeats!'

The two goblins glared at Tob, who went on scratching his head, now completely at a loss.

''Tisn't never me what does the housekeepin',' he said lamely.

'Grrr! Sphttt!' spat the goblins at him scornfully and started to scramble round, snuffing in the corners, scratching at the walls, trying to tear up the floorboards, growing more and more frenzied as each attempt yielded nothing, not a shawl, not a crumb, not a bottle, not a dish.

'Hi, you! She'll do us if you don't find something!' whispered Thrum-eye as he passed Tob. 'Where's your Mam keep her skirts?'

'She don't never wear skirts.'

'Coats then—you pimple-head!'

'She don't never wear coats.'

'Vesties then—you goat sucker!'

'She don't never wear vesties.'

'Don't she never eat neither?' The two goblins mocked Tob's way of speaking and drew up threateningly one on each side of him, blowing their cold vicious whispers down his ears.

'What d'you s'pose she'd want to eat for, you great gobble-gabies you!—or wear skirties or vesties or what-nots?' Tob answered with disgusted scorn. 'She isn't never a big stoopid princess nor a pair o' dirty little scratchy goblings wi' contrairy eyes!'

Tob could never remember clearly what happened during the next few minutes. Everything seemed to be whirling round in confusion, the coals from the fires were dancing across the room, the branches were slapping the walls, the floor was heaving, the princess was bellowing, the goblins screeching, they were all being tossed about from ceiling to floor, banging their heads and backs alternately. Then the movement became less violent and the house settled down into a regular swaying motion like a ship in a rough sea.

Tob sat up and rubbed his head. 'Now see what you've fair done been an' gone an' done!' he exclaimed angrily.

The goblins had been tossed into a corner, where they sat clutching each other fearfully and looking at Tob with awe. Thrum-eye's eyes were like two black rat holes, and Pin-eye's eyes looked as though they would pop right out of his head.

'Help me! Help me!' moaned the princess. 'I am battered to death and undone! My crown! My crown! My jewels and my robes! I am famished! I am famished! Oh, my bracelets and my boots! Loss and confusion! Treason and betrayal! No supper! No bed!'

She would have gone on as long as she could have found words to wail with had not Tob silenced her sharply:

'Bide still!' he commanded. ''Tis you what done it wi' your moanin's an' your discontentments an' your skirties an' your vesties an' such! Bide still! Or 'tis I that'll rattle the teeth out what's in your wicked skulls! Bide still!'

And bide still they did. The princess buried her face in the folds of her sodden clothes and the goblins crept abjectly under her skirts. Tob contemplated them for a time and felt almost sorry for them, but he wondered too whatever the house was up to. He did not trust it and it was still stumping along deliberately although it was now going much more slowly. He crept towards one window and peeped out through the hole in the shutter. It was too dark to see anything at all. He looked towards the princess and could see one eye watching him. The coals had settled back into the hearths and the eye glinted balefully in their light. He held up one paw threateningly and said 'Sh!' loudly. The eye disappeared. Just then the movement stopped and the house seemed to settle downwards slowly as though it had folded its legs underneath itself and was going to rest. Tob crept away from the window and sat down by the crown in the middle of the room.

Well, there the four of them were inside the strange little house, wet, cold, hungry and afraid, not having an idea of what was to become of them. The princess was afraid because it was all so strange and she began to think that Tob was a magician with his measuring rod and his strange way of talking and his ability to toss her about so roughly when he was angry. And nobody had ever been rude to her before, they would have been hashed up at once if they had tried, and it made her feel unprotected and forlorn. By now, she sadly thought, she should have been tucked up comfortably in bed, with three hot-water bottles and goblin slaves to sing to her in case she could not go to sleep. She began to cry and her big body heaved with sobs.

'Sh!' exclaimed Tob fiercely. Her sobs subsided and soon gave place to snoring. Merciful sleep had come to the princess.

Pin-eye and Thrum-eye were afraid because they did not know whatever the princess would do to them for failing to find supper and dry clothes or a nice bed with hot-water bottles. They kept as still as crouching cats under her skirt, not daring to relax until her snoring penetrated the sodden clothes and with relief they too fell asleep. Even bad goblins are sometimes afraid.

Tob was afraid because he did not really know whether the house was a friend or an enemy or where it had taken them. It had, after all, tempted him into this alarming adventure and it might have other things in store for him. He did not go to sleep but sat very still and tense, listening to the princess's snores.

Dawn had come and a clear glint of light was showing through the shutters. The princess had stopped snoring and was moaning mournfully in her sleep.

''Tis now or 'tisn't never,' thought Tob desperately. He gave one last look at the crown lying beside him, its pink and white jewels shining faintly in the new light.

'Our Mam don't never wear crowns,' he thought sadly and crept silently towards the door. Just as he was reaching for the latch a sepulchral whisper from behind him said: 'Wait! I'm coming too!' and he looked round to see the stalky eyes of Pin-eye waving to and fro at floor level. The princess stirred. Tob felt desperate.

'If you breathes so much as a teeny wink or lifts one of your dirty scaly little paws—I'll fix you like as you'll be ate right up, nasty wiggly little eyes an' all!' he whispered fiercely and the eyes withdrew. Tob quickly opened the door and slipped outside. He took one great glorious breath of cold morning air, dropped on his four feet and bolted.

He bolted wildly without looking where he was going and if you had been watching him you would have guessed that a swarm of hornets was after him. He crashed through bramble bushes and plunged over brooks and banged into tree trunks, he jumped and shied like a frightened horse and his course was like a snipe's on a windy day. He had no idea where he was going, in fact he did the stupidest thing he could have done, he went in a complete circle and ended up exactly where he had started—just outside the front door of the little house. *But the house was no longer there.*

He was exhausted, and lay there panting, and when he was recovered enough to look about him he saw his own wild frenzied track stretching away in front of him, with his own paw marks stamped violently into the ground. He looked behind and there were no tracks at all, only a quiet patch of grass and four indentations where the legs of the house must have rested.

So many curious things had happened to him in the last two days that as he made his way soberly down the hill towards his home, Tob began to wonder whether he had dreamed them all. He hoped that this was so because he felt ashamed of the part that he had played. He had started off so proud and full of hopes, he had been led by his own conceit into being stupid and reckless, fearfully rude and rather unkind. And he had been startled at his own behaviour. Never before had he ordered people about, he had always left that to Cob. He wondered how the damp and hungry princess and her pair of miserable retainers were faring and what tricks would be played on them by that unpredictable little house. The more he thought of the adventure the less he liked it and he hurried down the zigzags and across the stone bridge where the walnut shells were still lying scattered about. He plunged into the cloud which was still lying in the valley and never stopped to play on its edge or give a thought to the song which he had made. Soon he reached the mouth of the den and Father Bear leaned over and caught him two tremendous cuffs. He did not like the cubs to be out alone at night, and two nights out was a sin. Feeling very sore both inside and out Tob burrowed down into the moss and fell into an exhausted sleep.

When he woke the next morning Mother Bear was sharing out honeycomb among the cubs. Tob took his share and turned to carry it outside to eat it in the sunshine.

As he reached the door of the den his insides seemed to melt and his legs folded up like concertinas underneath him. There was the house, standing just below him on the edge of the wood, looking exactly as though it had been built there and had always stood in just that place, and the smoke was streaming away from its chimneys on that calm and sunny morning.

'Our Tob's that sick!' called Nob to her mother.

Mother Bear looked at him with an experienced eye.

'Didn't never oughter eat frogs, he didn't,' she remarked, and went on breaking up the honeycomb.

Tob stared at the house and the house stared back at him. After a long time one of the holes in the shutters closed very slowly and then opened again. The house had winked. Then a tiny crack appeared in the door and it started to open very, very slowly. Tob was terrified of what he might see, but he could not move his eyes from the expanding crack, he was mesmerized and had to look. The crack grew wider and wider and the door was right open; the house was empty and the branches were piled back neatly into the corner. Very, very slowly, the door closed again, the smoke started to go up calm and straight, and the house began to move almost imperceptibly back among the trees. It seemed to be beckoning Tob, although afterwards when he thought of it he could never make out how this could be, but as it moved so he had to follow, slowly, slowly into the wood, until they were both quite hidden by the bushes and sitting in a little green dell all by themselves.

Tob broke a long awed silence. 'How come she do be gone?' he asked.

'I spilled her out by the Cat Gate. The zigzags made her very sick. It was like swallowing a corkscrew.'

'And them wipsy little toughs, them as had contrairy eyes?'

'I spilled them out too.'

Tob considered and then went on. 'For why did you done draw that there picture what made me do it?'

The house screwed its shutters up in a puckish way and its chimneys looked like two wicked little horns, but it did not answer.

'You did oughter bide still and not make no more trouble!' said Tob sternly.

'Bide still!' exclaimed the house crossly, suddenly losing its puckish look. 'Why, I'm the only one that does bide still ever at all! And all the rest of you gallop around like mad March hares in moonlight! Bide still indeed! Why, what do you suppose I've been teaching myself all this time and what do you suppose I'm doing when you tear past and make such a wind that you almost blow the smoke out of my chimneys! Look at the trees! Look at the grass! Look at yourself! All at full gallop fair blowing my top off! I've a job to keep up with you, wasting my time, whirling about as you do! Why, if you really learned to keep still you'd know a darnside more than you do now!'

Tob, sitting stolidly on his little patch of grass, found this speech surprising. He looked round at the leaves and branches which seemed so serene and motionless in the calm air.

''Tisn't never us as moves——' he began and then stopped. A new thought had struck him. Perhaps after all his ideas were all wrong. Perhaps when he thought he was walking along a road, it was really the road that was walking along him. And a zigzag road would be like a corkscrew— no wonder the princess had been sick—and perhaps if he could learn to walk in the right direction at the right pace, he would be learning to stay quite still. He looked at the house with new respect, but this idea was too complicated for discussion without a great deal more thought. He changed the subject.

"'Twas so as I did answer them riddles correct an' proper,' he said, 'but 'twasn't never myself what done say it.'

'If you think that you can understand everything that comes out of your mouth or everything that goes on in your head, you are more foolish than I took you for,' answered the house scornfully. 'And anyway, how do you expect your brain to work at all when you will buzz around all the time like a drunken blue bottle on a summer day? I'm tired of your whirling! I'm going to keep still! Whirl yourself!'

Tob watched the smoke which had been blowing among the tree tops straighten itself until it was upright again. He was still sitting there stolidly on the grass, but somehow the distance between himself and the house was widening.

'Hi!' it called just before disappearing between the tree trunks. 'Hi! You've forgotten something!'

It landed at his feet. It was his measuring rod, which he must have dropped somewhere or left inside the house. Fixed to its top was a thin piece of bark paper and on it was written in sticky pink ink:—

TUP YATS

# The Music Lesson

Skyboy could think of nothing but his new pipe. He whittled and he fiddled and he blew, and he whittled again and blew again until even Thunder began to get impatient, so that he stood up and yawned and lay down again, and stared at him hard through his bush of hair in the hope that he would come away and do something different. But this particular pipe pleased Skyboy so much he could not leave it alone. It looked the same as all his other pipes; it had the same number of stops, but there was something about the tone and the soft fluty voice of it that filled him with a frenzied anxiety to perfect it. It was so beautiful already he felt he had perfection within his grasp and he would not let it slip. So he went on whittling and fiddling and blowing and Thunder curled up again resignedly and went to sleep.

Then with a great shout Skyboy leaped up. 'I've got it! I've got it! Listen to this!' he cried. He put the pipe to his lips and played a tune that was so lilting and merry that the big dog lifted his head and held it first on one side and then on the other, then, lolling his pink tongue as though he were laughing, he jumped to his feet and started to dance, scuttering his paws among the leaves and whirling round and round like a spindle.

When Skyboy could no longer blow for laughing he shouted: 'Dance again! Dance again, Thunder! See what you can do with this one!' He changed to a soft swaying tune, then to a galumphing gallop, then again to a frenzied rushing up and down the scale, and each time Thunder changed his steps to suit the music, joining more and more in the ridiculous fun, his tongue lolling and his body swaying and leaping and twirling until, bursting with the absurdity of it all, the two of them raced off between the trees and collapsed in a tangled jumble of arms and legs and fur down a soft bank of earth at the edge of the woodland. Skyboy rolled over and over till his mouth and clothes were full of leaves and grit and he was quite helpless with laughter. Thunder could not laugh, but he grinned all over as only dogs can grin.

'This is no day for chopping firewood or carrying water or caring for sheep,' said Skyboy emphatically. 'This is the day of the pipe. I am going to do exactly what I want to do, which is mostly nothing. I will wander, I will make music and you, Thunder, can dance. What do you think of that?'

Thunder wagged his behind, and Skyboy shook the twigs and leaves out of his clothes and spat the grit out of his mouth. 'Come on,' he said. 'Let's go.'

Thunder still wagged but did not move.

'Oh, come on!' said Skyboy again. 'Don't you want to?'

'You know quite well that there are five new lambs already and lots more coming. What will happen to them if there is nobody to look after them?'

'What are the ewes for if they can't look after their own children?'

'Ewes are shockingly stupid careless animals. They always need somebody to help.'

'Just this once!' pleaded Skyboy. 'I'll play and you can dance. I can't always be good. Do another dance, do now, and I'll play a lovely tune!'

'No,' said Thunder firmly. 'I like to dance a bit sometimes, but not all day. I want to sit with a new-born lamb between my paws and contemplate the universe. I know what you feel, I used to feel like that myself. But not now. You go. "I will dance it on the feet of my friend."' He quoted an old dog's proverb often used by parent dogs when they are tired of playing with their puppies and want them to go away and play by themselves. He turned round, clambered up the bank and started to trot back between the trees, and Skyboy knew from the look of his woolly quarters that it was no good calling to him or trying to get him to change his mind.

'You are an old bog-slogger!' he exclaimed in disgust. 'But I suppose you are right and I am wrong, but I just can't be good always and this time I'm going to do just what I want.' He danced off in the opposite direction, playing little airs on his pipe, lamenting the dullness of old age and arguing the pros and the cons of a spring day spent as a truant in the woods. His mood of wild jubilation returned, old age was dismissed, the pros had it and he jigged away merrily, forgetting Thunder, forgetting the lambs, forgetting everything that he should have been doing in the glorious fun of just being himself. He made up steps and tunes as he went along until he was drunk with sound and movement and felt more wildly happy than ever he had felt in his life before.

He was dancing through open parkland with clumps of dark cedars, birches in their newest green and stretches of flowery grassland in between. Hills arose on either side and, as he went, they became more steep and rocky, and the sound of his piping bounced back from off their sides as though there were now three pipes instead of only one. To invite the echoes he ran from one side of the valley to the other, and the mocking shadows of his music chased him to and fro as he went. Presently he grew hungry and stopped to feel for the lump of bread he usually carried in his pocket. He sat down to eat and, while he was eating, two young hares hopped out of the grass nearby and started to play. 'I will make them dance like Thunder,' he thought, so he played a hoppetty jiggetty tune and the hares got up on their hind legs and leaped and somersaulted and turned catherine wheels and frog-jumped and contorted themselves fantastically, and as a hare is better than any other animal at that mad kind of fun, it was a splendid sight to see. Skyboy played until his lips ached and he could contain himself no longer and burst into a great shout of laughter. The hares leaped outwards and away from each other in two great semi-circular arcs and disappeared in opposite directions.

'Oh, come back, do!' cried Skyboy and started to play again, but they were gone racing off madly out of sight, so he got up and continued on his way.

His meal had not sobered him in the least. He went racing and jumping and leaping the bushes, splashing through streams, swinging on branches, losing his cap, tearing his stockings, cavorting wildly, madder than the maddest March hare. Something was welling up inside him and bursting from his throat, his limbs were tingling and the tingles were running out of their tips as though he was on fire; he ran his fingers through his hair and it crackled like a flame. Great, irrepressible, tumultuous longings and ideas were pounding round and round in his head, exploding to get free and making him dizzy with delight. His feet could hardly stay on the ground, he might have flown away and trodden the white clouds or soared off rapturously along the wind. And all the time he whistled on his pipe, shrill mad little tunes brimming over with ecstasy and joy. And, of course, he did not look or care where he was going or give a rap as to whether he was lost or not. He reached a pine wood and threw himself down on the warm ground, caressed the earth and kissed it as though it had been his mother, took up armfuls of the needles and hugged them, threw them up so that they fell down over his head in a prickly shower, surrounding him with their delicious resinous smell as though they were embracing him in their turn. In fact, if you, in an ordinary practical everyday mood, had come upon Skyboy at that moment you would certainly have thought that he was a little mad, but if the spring had got into your bones as it had got into his, perhaps you would have understood what he was feeling.

He certainly did not understand himself. He was overcome with love for the earth, not the earth as a large abstract idea, but the earth as the honest dirt he picked up in his hands and all the trees that buried their roots in the dirt and the birds that sang in the branches of the trees and the flowers that grew under them and the rocks that sheltered the flowers. But all that he looked like was just a messy boy with pine needles in his hair.

Presently the sound of a stream penetrated the confusion of his thoughts and he sat up and listened. The pine needles had gone down inside his clothes and were pricking his skin, so he shook and scratched and stood on his head against a tree trunk to get rid of them. Then he went to investigate the stream, which was running half-hidden through a grove of sycamores nearby, not tall trees but spreading trees with twisted stems and branches bending close above the moving water. Inside the grove the light was mottled and broken, the stream ran over stones and little waterfalls and he sat down on a low flat branch and took out his pipe again and started to play. He wanted to imitate the stream and he stopped every now and then to listen to the voice of the water and try to repeat it on his pipe. It was not easy, the stream was so delicate and tinkly, his pipe too strident and fluty. And mixed up with the water sound was something like laughter which he could not imitate at all. He pushed his way up and down the side of the stream to find out what made the water laugh, but when he moved the laughter seemed to stop, so he sat down again on the branch to listen more carefully still. He trilled his pipe and a lizard ran out into the dappled sunlight on a rock in front of him and ripples ran down its tail in answer to the trilling ripples on his pipe. Another lizard appeared and another and another, and presently all their tails were rippling like water flowing across the rock. Here was something even better than the dance of the hares, and he went on playing and the lizards went on rippling until he could play no more and the lizards darted back into the crack from which they had appeared.

Skyboy leaned back and gasped with pure joy and the air was like wine drawn into his throat. Then he heard that laugh again and this time he was sure that the sound did not come from the water and he peered carefully among the leaves. He was so enclosed by branches that he could not see far, but his eyes came to rest on something that might have been a green face, but it was so mixed up with sun and shadow that he could not be sure that it was a face at all. He watched it for a while and sometimes it looked as though a face was there and sometimes it looked as though the sunlight was playing on a patch of leaves, and because he did not like the feeling of being watched, he crept out from under the sycamores and into an open space below the pine trees where he could see clearly all round him.

The sun was going down and his reckless mood was fading with the daylight. He knew that he was quite lost, and if he had wanted to turn for home he would not even have known in which direction to start. An hour before he would not have cared but now he started to look about and wonder what he should do. There was a rocky shelf behind the sycamore grove and an overhanging cliff which sheltered it on to which the low sun was blazing and turning the rocks blood red. Skyboy skirted the sycamore grove and climbed up on to the shelf, where he found a comfortable flat seat cut into the stone. The stream ran out of a narrow cleft in the rock beside him, hurrying by under his seat as clear and smooth as crystal, then breaking up to run in a dozen hurrying channels which joined again to enter the grove. He sat in the warm sunlight, glowing ruddy like the rocks and eating the remainder of his bread. Then he took out his pipe again and played softly to the setting sun.

He sat there while the light faded and the moon rose and threw the weirdest shadows across the cliff and down on to the sycamore grove, so that there was not a creature real or unreal that could not have been imagined moving about there at some time or another during that enchanted night. The rocks kept the heat of the sun, and Skyboy felt warm and content. He dozed a little but not very much, and every now and then he would play on his pipe and imagine that he heard things dancing very softly just below him. Before dawn he was overcome with drowsiness; he laid his pipe down beside him, hunched up his knees, pillowed his head against them and fell asleep. A figure crept out of the sycamore grove, stole very softly up the edge of the stream, sidled cautiously underneath where Skyboy was sleeping and disappeared into the cleft in the rock out of which the stream was flowing.

Skyboy woke with a start because in his dreams he had

heard something scratching and scraping, something like dry skin rubbing against rock. He looked about him at the trees and the cliffs in the luminous early morning light. Wisps of cloud were curling among the pines and a few stars were perched in their topmost branches. A sleepy bird was chirping among the sycamores. He looked down for his pipe which he had placed beside him before going to sleep and suddenly he was stiff with fear. A thin green arm was reaching stealthily out of the cleft, and long green fingers were feeling across the rock towards his pipe. He could not move for awful fear, but watched the fingers close upon the pipe and slowly withdraw, the dry green skin scraping softly over the rock until arm, pipe and hand disappeared into the darkness out of which the spring was flowing.

A paralysis of terror held Skyboy until the sun had risen behind the cliff, throwing a great blue shadow out in front of him and lighting up the opposite hills in a blaze of clear morning light. Then the paralysis passed and a kind of caution of which he had known nothing the day before began to take control of him and he climbed very carefully down from his perch, even looking where he was putting his feet, and watching apprehensively for any sign of movement from the cleft. He was resolutely making up his mind to a sober steady slog for home, hoping that he had not lost himself so successfully in yesterday's lunatic journey that he could not find his way, when a sound of the utmost sweetness fell on his ears and stopped him dead where he stood. He turned round to listen and the music stopped. He turned once more for home and there was the music again. There was no mistaking that it came from the cleft. He stood irresolute, torn between the comforting safety of home and the unutterable longing which welled up inside him as he listened to that music. For a moment he hesitated like a reed blown to and fro in the wind, then he turned and climbed back up the rocks and stood peering and listening at the black opening of the cleft while the clear water of the stream flowed by underneath his feet.

He must have stood there for five or even for ten minutes and there was no sound but the gushing of the water and his own blood pulsing in his temples. But he knew that he must follow that music, however unwillingly and at whatever cost, and he was only waiting for some sign that would guide him. And then it came again, very faint and low, but clear enough to draw him through the dark cleft and right into the blackness that lay behind.

To enter he had to step into the stream and wade with one hand on each wall to guide him. Then the walls opened out and he lost his guiding holds, but as his eyes became used to the darkness he saw that the stream held a faint light of its own and he could trace its course across the floor of the cave. The water was icy cold and he was shivering, so he climbed out and groped his way along beside the luminous water. Other things in the cave were shining faintly too, there were long stalactites like hanging icicles, and above his head the roof glowed like frozen clouds reflecting dawn. Silent falls of glistening rock cascaded without movement down the walls, and the stream fanned out in a translucent bed which mirrored the pale mysterious sights above and beside it. The longer Skyboy was in the cave, the more he was able to see and even his own dim irregular shadow was moving beside him like a companion.

He reached the birthplace of the stream where it gushed strongly from the floor of the cave, the welling water catching a lustre on its surface and looking like a petalled flower on a luminous stem as it flowed away into the dark. But now that his watery guide had come to an end, he did not know which way to turn. He could go back along the stream and find his way out of the cave, but he was still haunted by the music, so with his arms in front of him and treading very cautiously he groped towards the farther wall, hoping to find another way out or a way farther in. He reached the wall and felt with his hands along it, but he could find no break in it, so he returned to the spring, angry at the loss of his pipe but unwilling to give up his quest so soon. Suddenly the music broke out again quite loud and startling, above him and not far away. It was a tantalizing evocative tune which bounced and junketed all round the cave and back again, shattering itself against the stalactites and disappearing in airy trills somewhere up in the faintly visible roof. Skyboy turned first this way then that, trying desperately to trace where the sound was coming from or catch a glimpse of the player.

'Where are you?' he cried and his own voice echoed round and round the cave as though there were six boys calling instead of only one. There was silence again and then one impudent 'Pip!' on the pipe, too small and sudden to give much clue to where it came from.

'Who are you and where are you?' shouted Skyboy angrily. 'Give me back my pipe or I'll fight you for it when I find you!'

'Find me first,' mocked a voice.

'Come out into the light then. I can't see you in here!'

'Not I!' said the voice and struck up another merry tune which rocketed round and round, confusing its own tracks so successfully that Skyboy had no idea whether it came from this side or that side, from high up or low down. He swallowed his anger and remained silent.

'Hi!' laughed the voice. 'Don't you like my music? I'm off now. If you're not a coward you'll follow me!'

There was a triumphant arpeggio on the pipe which faded

suddenly as pipe and player seemed to turn a corner or go through a door or exit of some kind. Skyboy felt hot anger rush to his face, he would not lose his pipe or be treated so insolently no matter how sweetly the piper played. He must catch this exasperating thief and force him to give up not only the pipe but the secret of his playing, for every note that he had uttered had penetrated Skyboy to his very marrow and had melted and drawn his soul from him like spring rain drawing the flowers from the earth or sunlight melting frost. He groped again feverishly backwards and forwards over the walls of the cave, above his head and down to his feet. There was no door that he could find, but at the third try he felt what he thought might be the first step of a rough staircase at the level of his shoulders. He scrambled up, cutting his knees and bruising his shins; then, hanging on desperately, he pulled himself to where a draught in his face told him that there was some sort of hole, through which he pushed on hands and knees.

'Are you there?' he shouted into the blackness when the floor levelled off and he felt secure from slipping backwards.

'Pip!' answered the pipe and he scrambled on, not thinking, not caring, only intent on catching up with that terrible wonderful music.

'Don't be in such a scrambling hurry!' called the voice just in front of him. 'If you're really coming after me you've got an awfully long way to come. Save your shoe leather!' And then, after a pause—'Only come if you want to. You can still see your way back if you look over your shoulder. It wouldn't take you long to get back into the sunshine. Pip!'

Skyboy did look back and did see a pale opening and he could still hear the noise of the stream welling up from its spring. He had never much liked caves or darkness, but he gritted his teeth and made no answer, pushing his way on, sometimes on hands and knees, sometimes shuffling along with his hands in front of him, continuously tripping and floundering against unseen obstacles. He could hear footsteps in front of him and they seemed to be running gaily and smoothly away into the distance.

'If he can run then I can crawl!' he thought grimly, confident that a few more yards would bring him through the evil passage and out into some open space beyond. To encourage him a little light did start to filter in from above his head and he was able to see well enough to stand up without fear of knocking his head, but then he found that he could not keep his feet because the walls and floor were coated with a thin film of ice and he was slipping and falling at every step. He was bitterly cold and the cuts on his hands and legs ached painfully.

The passage, which had led an irregular course, now straightened into a long narrow corridor dimly visible for a great distance and glistening in its coat of ice. As Skyboy turned into this corridor he thought he saw a figure disappear at the far end. It had moved so quickly that he could not be sure, but the glimpse encouraged him to struggle on, though for him there seemed no end to the passage or else the end was being drawn away continually so that he could not reach it. He began to hear a snuffling and a panting behind him, he stopped to listen several times and when he stopped the panting stopped too. He scrambled on in a panic, feeling hemmed in by terrors, unable to go back and unable to reach anything in front. The panting grew louder, it was just behind him, and, sweating with fear, he whipped round in a crouching position, determined to face whatever was pursuing him. A monstrous shape leaped at him out of the gloom smothering him as he struck out wildly with his bare fists, battering at the empty air and the menacing form of his own shadow, which flailed back at him frantically with impotent insubstantial blows. He wiped the sweat from his face and covered his eyes with his hands to shut out his own terrors, and when he opened them again he was at the end of the passage and a tall doorway stood in front of him, hung with heavy black curtains.

For a time no courage was left in him, and he stood looking at the curtains or staring back fearfully at the icy corridor through which he had come. Then because the unknown could hardly be more terrifying than what he had just encountered, he put out his hand to draw the curtains. He laid hold of a fold and it was clammy to the touch and resisted as he pulled, closing again of its own volition as he pushed his way in. There seemed to be fold upon fold of curtain, airless and cold and clinging, so that before he was through he was gasping for breath and half-suffocated by the loathsome hangings. He found himself standing in a gloomy hall dimly lighted through a high circular opening which reached up and up until it curved away out of sight. There was an old stale smell, and all round the hall hung the heavy curtains so that now he could not see where he had come in or any way by which he could get out.

He stared about all round him and then sat down in the middle of the hall, hoping to hear some guiding signal from the pipe telling him which way to go, but as soon as he had sat down and his eyes were on a lower level he saw something which froze up his blood and kept him sitting as silent and as motionless as a stone.

Now he knew of what sinister cloth the curtains were made, because there, underneath them, now at the level of his own eyes, was a circle of fierce staring faces with merciless beady eyes and sharp white teeth protruding from their mouths. The curtains were formed by the wings of hundreds of gigantic bats hanging head downwards round the sides of the hall. Their clawed toes clung to their perches like curtain hooks and their furry heads were shrouded in the black folds of their own uncanny membranes.

Presently something like a draught blew along the line of folded wings, they rasped together drily and the bats shuffled and fidgeted on their hooks. They did not seem to be speaking to each other, but some of them turned their heads and chattered their sharp teeth and twisted and cocked their large ears as though they might have been arguing or making up their minds about something. Then, without warning, each bat unhooked one clammy wing and shot it forward across the floor, and before Skyboy had time to realize what was happening, he was held in a vice of hooks, the firmly imprisoned centre of a sinister circle of out-stretched wings and glittering eyes.

Now that there was absolutely nothing that he could do to help himself, Skyboy almost stopped being frightened. He closed his eyes as tight as he could and with an enormous effort of will, he imagined himself back at home outside the cottage door with a very big steaming plate of pease porridge on his lap. With the other half of his mind he was wondering what it would be like to be all in little pieces lying in a circle round the bats' hall, one piece under each bat. The two thoughts kept him occupied for what seemed a very long time and when he opened his eyes again, to his surprise, he was still all in one piece, and one by one the bats were unhooking themselves from his coat, with-drawing their outstretched wings and hooking them up again above their heads. Skyboy felt sure that he was seeing things wrongly, so he closed his eyes once more, but when he looked again he was even more astonished to see that all the bats were fast asleep. They were swaying gently on their hooks, the fierceness had gone out of their expressions and their furry faces with their large trumpet ears looked almost benevolent. Skyboy stared and stared and thanked

his stars for this unexpected turn of events, but even so—
how was he going to escape? The folded membranes of the
bats' wings enveloped the walls and any attempt he made to
push through might rouse them again to their former fierce
mood, and he could hardly expect his luck to hold a second
time. So all he could do was to wait and he hunched himself
as small as he could in the middle of the floor and waited.

The light coming through the high chimney above had
always been dim, but now it was becoming dimmer and
the bats began to stir again. Presently one bat unhooked
itself and with a great tempest of wings started to spiral
upwards until the noise of its going faded high up in the
distance. Then another bat followed and another and
another, and each one made a great wind as it went so that
Skyboy clutched himself desperately for fear that he might
be blown about the floor in the violent draught of their
flight. Then everything was silent and dark and he could
not tell whether all the bats had gone or whether some of
them were still hanging in their ominous wrappings round
the walls.

'You can come out now,' said the voice suddenly,
followed by a few notes of melody on the pipe.

'Are they all gone?' whispered Skyboy. He was angry
that the voice should sound so cheerful and matter-of-fact
after all that he had been through.

'Oh, yes, they have all gone, and even if they hadn't they
couldn't hear you talking. You can talk as loud as you like.
Didn't I play them to sleep most beautifully?'

'You played them to sleep! You didn't make a sound!
You wouldn't have cared if I'd been torn limb from scrag,
you horrid little thief you!'

'I *did* play them to sleep, or they *would* have torn you limb
from scrag, stupid! Only you couldn't hear, nor can the
bats hear you. They think you're deaf and dumb and you

think they're deaf and dumb and really I don't know who's right. But I shouldn't dawdle about if I were you, they'll be back when they've completed their missions.'

'Missions!' thought Skyboy angrily to himself. 'Whoever heard of bats having missions! Missions to eat people alive or suck their blood or terrify the life out of them!'

'Oh, no, you're quite wrong,' answered the voice as though it had heard exactly what Skyboy was thinking. 'They have very important missions, carrying supersonic cadences and that sort of thing which other people can't do. But come along now, you've only started your journey and there is a terrible lot to learn before you are a real musician.'

Skyboy pulled himself up indignantly and stumbled off in the direction of the voice. Becoming a real musician indeed! He did not see that this miserable chase after his own pipe had got anything to do with it. But he did not want to be in the bats' hall when the bats came back. And he was right under the spell of that voice and of the music that it made. He had no choice but to go on.

'Oh, it's dark and I'm lost and I'm far under the world and how can I ever get out into the light again?'

If the voice had intended to make an end of Skyboy it could have done so easily by leading him over a precipice in the dark or luring him into another conclave of strange fierce animals, so, knowing that he had no power left to protect himself, he had stepped out with all the boldness that he could muster, but now for a long time he had heard no voice and no music, he had felt no limit to the darkness all round him, he had sensed no glimmer of light. His feet grew as heavy as stones, his legs stiffened and grew cold, his hands were icy and weighed him down towards the ground. He stumbled and fell and lay down where he fell, and a trance-like sleep enveloped him, and he dreamed that he had become part of the rock on which he lay, far down in the middle of the earth where no light or sound ever came and which had lain there buried since the beginning of time. He was heavy, hard, cold and immovable, he was just a contour in a stone, a forgotten part of the forgotten roots of a forgotten world.

But out of rocks all strength has come and rocks contain the seed and germ of power secretly inside them, waiting for that conjunction of mysterious forces that will release the tremendous universal life hidden in their hard dark bodies, the sparks of fire, the origin of animals, the origin of plants, precious gems, gold and silver, atoms imprisoned for a million million years, constellations and suns. And all this seemed to be contained in his poor lost stony body lying there forgotten in the dark. But just as power cannot remain for ever hidden in the rock, so he began to feel a great groaning and cracking like monstrous birth pangs, his limbs started to separate themselves from the stone, his body poured with human sweat and he felt himself surging upwards on a vast roaring like a flame. And all at once he found that he was himself again, and himself on an ordinary grey morning, lying on an ordinary rock, and the land around him was ordinary with trees and grass. And by his side, cross-legged on the grass sat a boy and in his hand he held the stolen pipe.

Everything about the boy was green. His hair was green, his skin was greenish, his clothes were green, he looked in fact as though he lived always under some kind of green light. Greenness suited him, he seemed to have acquired it naturally, as some people acquire a tan. He was a wild-looking boy with a mop of straight unruly hair and a thin face with fine wrinkles at the corners of his eyes, which were darkly ringed and wide and haunting.

They looked at each other for a long time and at last Skyboy broke the silence. 'So you're the thief who stole my pipe and led me into all that!' He did not speak angrily or reproachfully, only with a kind of wonder at seeing someone not altogether unlike himself who had known his way through all those underground terrors and who had managed somehow to lead them both out again into a familiar kind of a world.

'When I heard you playing in the sycamore grove,' said the green boy, 'I liked you. You played very beautifully to that brook, so beautifully I knew that I could teach you to play more beautifully still.'

'It seems a queer sort of way to teach people to play music, scrambling through awful icy passages, being nearly torn to bits by bats and being buried down under the ground. Anyway, I don't want any more of it.' Skyboy rubbed his limbs to make sure that he had left nothing of himself deep down in the underworld or brought anything belonging to the underworld up with him. 'No, I don't want any more of it,' he repeated ruefully, looking at his tattered clothes and cut hands and knees.

'Oh, you don't have to,' said the green boy, 'but you'll be sorry if you don't. All that I'm doing is to show you how, which is easier than finding out for yourself, not that you'd even try.' His green eyes looked far away into the distance and he twiddled the pipe in his fingers.

Skyboy screwed up his face and rumpled his hair. He felt afraid, but he did not want the green boy to know.

'What else would I have to do?' he asked.

'Well, first I'll tell you what you've already done. You've learned what it is to be afraid, you've learned what it is to be alone and you've learned a lot about beginnings. That's not a bad start.'

'What else?'

'Well, there's so much,' said the green boy. 'It's difficult to know where to go on from. Things like tying up stars and loosing them again, clothing the sea with clouds and prisoning it behind rocks, ordering the morning and the evening to come and go and the ice to freeze up and the water to burst out.'

'It's nonsense to think I can do those things,' said Skyboy in a practical tone, relieved to find that further lessons were out of the question. 'Why, nobody can do things like that; you can't, I can't, nobody can.'

'Not *do* them, no, but know about them—understand them by being part of them. I can't explain, but I'll give you a simple example. Listen!'

The green boy held the pipe to his lips and started to play. The tune was liquid, rocking, gurgling, gentle and full of quiet laughter, very much what Skyboy had tried to play when he was sitting among the sycamores at the beginning of this adventure. Only it was much, much better. It really was a brook put into sound. Skyboy felt his hair lift up and ripple out behind him and he watched his feet stream off down the rock and over the meadow. He tumbled down a waterfall and flowed off through a wood. Trout hid under the shadows of the banks at his sides and moorhens splashed noisily away into the rushes. A heron stood solitary beside a pool and a cloud of gnats jigged and danced above a backwater.

'You see that's what it's like to BE a brook.' The green boy had stopped playing and Skyboy was back again on his rock, surprised that not even his feet were wet. 'You couldn't have known that before, could you?'

'I suppose not,' said Skyboy. 'It wasn't really like what I imagined.'

'Well, you see, that's just the point. Brooks know. People don't. People sometimes *think* they know but their ideas are usually wrong. Now let's try something else just to show you——'

He blew on the pipe again and Skyboy's feet slid gently over the edge of the rock and rooted themselves firmly in the ground. His body became upright and he seemed to have too many arms, they stretched outwards and upwards and his fingers spread and grew, and what had happened to his head he had no idea. A cold wind blew through his branches, which were as bare as driftwood, and patches of snow lay round his ankles. He was shut away somewhere inside himself, safe behind the walls of bark and wood. Then he found that he was swelling and swelling and swelling, great pulsings and surgings were forcing themselves up from his feet, the snow had gone, warm sun was shining on him, rain was trickling down his fingers. The swelling and surging spread all over him and when there was no more room for it to swell and surge any more, it lodged in agonizing points along his arms and at the tips of his fingers. He was bursting and soaring upwards, he did not know whether this was pain or ecstasy and suddenly he was accomplished and fulfilled and covered all over with green leaves of the utmost delicacy and starred with sweet-smelling flowers.

'I won't take you through to the autumn, it's a little sad,' said the green boy. 'You can do that another time.'

Skyboy was back again on the rock rubbing his arms and his fingertips. 'That hurt!' he said.

'Of course it hurt. Nearly all nice things do hurt. But now when you sit and watch things coming out in the spring you'll not just say 'How pretty!' or 'How does it happen?' but you'll *know* there's all that agony and all that ecstasy going on around you in every twig and bud and blade of grass. And it will all go into your music.'

'There seems an awful lot to learn.'

'Oh, you won't learn it all or anything like. If you did, you'd never go home again and you'd turn green like me. In fact, you're getting a little bit green already.'

Skyboy looked ruefully at his hands and arms. He seemed to have grown terribly thin and rather green as well.

'I don't want to go green,' he said. 'I think I really want to go home, but I would like to take my pipe with me.'

'Not yet! not yet!' said the green boy, clutching the pipe tightly. 'Let me have it a little bit longer. You can't waste all that you have done——' and he drew away from Skyboy.

'Oh, all right, all right. I promise I won't take it yet. Only please stay with me, because I don't know where I am. And please don't make me be any more things just now. I'm tired and I'm beginning to feel too wise to be real.'

Skyboy slid down off the rock as he spoke and snuggled into the grass and soon he was asleep. The green boy did not sleep but sat and watched him with his strange haunted eyes or stared away into the distance. An hour or two later they were walking side by side over the meadows, and if you had seen them together just then you might have thought that they were brothers. They were really growing remarkably alike.

'When can I play my pipe again?' asked Skyboy, who had stuck loyally to his promise and had made no attempt to take the pipe.

'You must learn about the discords first,' answered the green boy. 'So far you've only had some of the terrible and beautiful bits. Now you must have some of the angry, ugly bits as well.'

'Don't let there be any more caves.'

'You'll see what you will see. It's down under again, I'm afraid, but I won't leave you this time—that is not unless you don't do what you are told.'

There were many rocks in front of them, all jumbled in heaps and scattered down a hillside like the remains of a ruined city. They passed under a heavy stone gateway and turned immediately into an unlighted passage leading steeply downwards. Skyboy, whose dislike was growing strongly for any place out of sight of the day, followed with extreme unwillingness. He badly wanted to turn back but the green boy said urgently, 'Hurry! Hurry! Once in we must go through with it. If we hesitate, neither of us will have the courage. Hold my hand, I know the way.'

'Whatever can we be coming to if even he is afraid? And how much more of this hurrying through awful dark places?' But Skyboy found the feel of the green boy's hand wonderfully comforting, although the thin dry fingers were now his one contact with reality as everything was as pitchy black again as ever it had been before. Soon they could hear a dull metallic clanging which grew louder and louder until the din became so overwhelming that it seemed to be another element, more hostile even than the dark. Dull red gleams of light started to flicker along the walls and the passage ended in a high gallery above a chasm which seemed to be compounded of leaping flames and deafening clangings. Skyboy thought his head was going to split, and he let go of his companion to clamp his hands tightly over his ears. The green boy mouthed one word at him—'Discords!'—and pointed down over the side of the gallery. Skyboy shuddered and peered into the chasm, and far below he saw giants with monstrous hammers beating on bars of metal lighted by the flames of a gaping furnace whose fury rose and fell in the draught of a demoniac bellows. The giants were sitting in two lines facing each other; between them ran a conveyor belt loaded with metal pieces and as the belt passed so each giant cracked his hammer down on the metal and the last giant in the line flung the battered pieces out into a pile. As fast as the pile was built it was torn down frantically by hundreds of small naked creatures who were hurrying all over the place, some rushing back with the battered pieces to fling them again on to the conveyor belt for another battering, some furiously working the bellows and roaring a vicious shanty as they worked, some madly fuelling the furnace, running up a sloping ladder with baskets on their heads and flinging themselves, baskets, fuel and all into the licking flames.

A scene of more horrible aimless confusion and noise could hardly have been imagined. Skyboy stared horror-struck, unable to take his eyes off the hellish sight, till he realized that the green boy was pulling at him urgently and signing to him to come. They ran down the length of the gallery and reached a steep iron staircase leading down into the inferno below. The metal of the staircase was hot and as he reached the top step Skyboy could smell the burning leather of his shoes. The green boy started to clamber down the steps and Skyboy's yell of 'NO! NO! Come back! Come back!' was lost in the terrible din. He was torn between terror of being left alone and terror of what was below him. The green boy turned and beckoned desperately and Skyboy started to tumble recklessly down the smoking stairway and pitched headlong into a crowd of the small black fuel carriers frantically hurrying to their suicidal doom. Queer little demon creatures they were, some with pig snouts, some with duck bills that clacked, some rolling along like animated pitchers, but all with the one idea of getting into the flames as quickly as they could. As they neared the hot breath of the furnace mouth Skyboy could see that they were all being blown out again up a sort of chimney where they appeared at the top encased in gleaming metallic bubbles which floated on to the fiery air and burst their contents out again apparently unharmed and battling and biting at each other in their frenzied efforts to return to the endless excruciating circle of labour.

Mesmerized by the madness and futility and noise, Skyboy might have got pushed on to the fuelling ladder if the green boy had not seized him by the back of his coat and flung him unceremoniously on to what seemed even worse —the conveyor belt which passed between the giants. He had only time to curl himself up tightly between two slabs of metal, close his eyes and his ears and wait for what he felt was the inevitable hammer-blow. 'Clang! Clang! Clang!' went the hammers all round him, then with a suddenness that was as violent as everything else concerned with this terrible place, he was flung out into silence, back into the outside world, and the green boy was flung out beside him.

Skyboy was convinced that he was dead. He lay still, angry and resentful and sure that he was as flat as a pancake. And he would have remained sure if he had not opened one eye and seen his own arm and hand lying in front of him looking much as they always looked. But still he did not move. He was angry. He was very angry. He was angry with the green boy for making him go through all this, he was angry with himself for being so easily led, he was furiously angry that such a hideous place should exist as that Chasm of Discords. And he was even more angry when he opened his eye a little farther and saw the green boy's left leg and foot just beside him looking unconcerned as far as a leg and foot can look unconcerned. In fact, at that moment, Skyboy really wished that he had been hammered flat just so that at last somebody could feel sorry for him. But as there was nobody to feel sorry for him he lay and felt sorry for himself and then after a time he rose slowly without a glance at the green boy and stalked off, looking as haughty and offended as he could. He went on until he hoped he was out of sight and then he looked up and down and round about, and he had not the slightest idea where he was or what he was going to do. He had lost his way, he had lost his pipe and he was still shattered by the noise and the clanging. He sat down and hid his face in his hands and his whole body was wracked with sobbing and he gave himself up to his grief without hindrance.

When the first storm of his emotion was passed, he found that he was holding something smooth and hard in one hand. He fingered it, not understanding at first, then wiped away his tears and looked at it. It was his pipe. And the green boy was sitting beside him. And large shining tears were running down his cheeks as well.

'I'm sorry,' he said, 'but it was worth it. You will play so beautifully now.'

'Well, it won't be because of you! You've done your best to get me lost or eaten up or buried alive or hammered flat or blinded or deafened!' Skyboy spoke as angrily as he could. He did not like to be found crying and he turned his face away and was silent for a long time until he was quite sure he would not cry any more. 'I don't understand,' he went on. 'Are you a friend or an enemy?'

'Mostly a friend,' answered the green boy rather sadly.

'Then why did you do it? Why didn't you warn me what was going to happen?'

'If I'd warned you what was going to happen, you'd never have come. I don't much like it myself.'

'You've done it all before?'

'Oh, yes,' and the green boy shrugged his thin shoulders.

They said no more, but Skyboy sat thinking deeply. Why was this strange boy willing to do all this and at the end willing to give him back the pipe? At first he had thought he was just a thief, then that he was mischievous and rather unkind, but now he could not make him out at all. He fingered the pipe absently and put it to his lips. And without thinking very much he began to play of all the beautiful and terrible things that he had experienced, the dark caves, the fierce bats, the loneliness, the fear, the brook, the bush that flowered, the Chasm of Discords and the strange green boy himself. And the sound of his playing was so exquisite that the ants scurried out of the earth and the butterflies stopped in their flight and the birds dropped out of the sky and the trees bent their branches towards him and they all listened. And when he stopped playing he put the pipe down beside him with a great sigh.

'Yes, it was worth it,' he said.

Then he looked at his hands, and they had grown long and thin and green and the skin on them was dry like the skin of the green boy. And he looked at the green boy and suddenly he saw himself. They had grown exactly alike.

'I can never go home like this,' he said. 'They wouldn't even know who I was.'

'That's the trouble,' said the green boy. 'We can't ever go home like this.'

And they held their hands and arms up against each other's and compared them and then laughed, not very happily because both of them felt rather sad.

'What shall I do?' said Skyboy, for much as he loved the music, he thought with a great pang of all the things that he loved at home, of his mother and his father and of Little-flame and Thunder and the sheep and lambs and the fields round the village.

'Well, there is a way of half going home,' answered the green boy rather sorrowfully. 'You can go home and forget and then sometimes come away and remember, but it isn't easy.'

'Oh,' said Skyboy, because he could find no words for what he was feeling, and he was torn in two inside himself because he wanted both things and he did not know which one he wanted most.

'Come,' said the green boy, 'we will go home and then you can decide.'

It was evening when they came to the village and the lights were coming out in the windows and the stars were coming out in the sky. They sat down on a tree stump about the distance of a field away and watched the lights and did not speak. And Skyboy took the pipe and he began to play, just an everyday lyrical song like the one a blackbird sings at nightfall, and a door opened and he saw his mother coming out to fetch some wood and she showed up clearly against the lighted space behind her. Thunder followed her and sniffed about by the woodpile, and a smell of newly baked bread came over the air. They stood up and looked at each other and they could read each other's eyes without speaking.

'Good-bye,' said the green boy and stepped back into the twilight.

Skyboy thought his heart was breaking—whatever he did his heart would break, whether he chose the warm patch of light behind him or the glimmering shape fading away from him. He was rooted where he stood, and all the strange happenings of the last hours—or days—he did not know which—rushed through his mind. He wrenched himself free and reached out desperately into the dark.

'At least take this!' he whispered, holding out the pipe in his hand. But the green boy had gone.

His mother called into the night. . . . 'Is that you at last? Wherever have you been all this time? You'll catch a fever to be sure—I can see the green light playing over the marshes.'

Thunder lifted his head and ran out to greet Skyboy,

and he turned towards the house and the door closed behind him.

His mother was quite right and Skyboy did have a fever and everybody said it was from staying out in the damp when the green light was playing over the marshes, and from going without proper food and from getting chilled. He looked exceedingly green and he was put to bed and made to keep warm and was given all sorts of special things to drink and very soon he was better.

He never told anybody what had happened to him and every now and then he would go off alone and wander about searching for somebody or behave as though he were lost himself. And he would play enchanting music in the woods, nobody had ever heard music like his before. And when he came home he was often ill again and people shook their heads and muttered. And never in his life was he completely cured, and what is more, he did not wish to be.

# Iced Bear and Spun Bear

'Go away, Hob! Go away, Hob! Go away, Hob!'

Hob was sitting on the summit of a grassy hill standing by itself among the tops of the trees which surrounded it like a green ocean. It was a favourite place of his. He could play that he was alone on an island, he could play that he was king of everything within sight, he could play that he was the only animal left alive in a great green flood of leaves. Today he was holding a small drum which Skyboy had made for him and he was beating out a rhythm on it, three shorts and a long, dogged, unvaried and terribly monotonous. Ever since he had got the drum his family had chanted at him rather unkindly, 'Go away, Hob! Go away, Hob!' so he had gone away with their chant in his head to beat it out to the sky and the tree-tops on this sweltering hot summer afternoon. There was no breath of wind and even the flies seemed too lazy to buzz.

'Go away, Hob! Go away, Hob! Go away, Hob!'

He closed his eyes and went on thumping, his thumps grew slower and slower, he drooped over his drum, pulled himself up, drooped again, then capitulated. Hob was asleep.

On the horizon there was a cloud and when it first appeared it was no bigger than Hob's drum and just about the same shape. It grew until it was as big as two drums and then as big as three drums, and then it trailed out skirts on each side, and gathered more skirts and voluminous petticoats which billowed and shouldered themselves up into the sky until they hid the sun and rolled forward in a threatening black mass, shutting out all light but for the long rays which escaped from its shining edges. The air grew hotter and hotter and breathless and still, except for a few nervous birds who started to cheep anxiously and flutter to their roosting places because they thought that night was falling. A restless sigh passed over the leaf ocean, running this way and then that. The trees trembled and groaned because they were heavy and tired with heat and full of unhappy foreboding.

The cloud was now as tall as a mountain, as black as ink and half as wide as a valley. Hitherto its only visible movement had been its swift growth up into the sky, but now a whirlpool of silver leaves started to form at its base, branches lashed and bent, twigs were torn free and spun up into the great misty pillar now hurrying over the leaf ocean, leaving a trail of torn tree-tops in its wake. When it reached the grassy hill where Hob lay, it hesitated, passing first to one side, then to the other, then gathering all its giant strength it tore with a mighty wind over the crest, picking up everything loose or breakable in its way, sweeping Hob and his drum into its ravening inside, which stretched up and up out of sight in the menacing sky.

Hob was wakened very rudely, his drum was snatched from him and he felt himself being sucked upwards at a terrifying rate. He was turned over and over, and soon he could not tell which was right way up and which was upside down, and all he could see were swirling masses of cloud. He was travelling so fast that the breath was almost snatched from him and he was no longer hot but growing very cold. His pace slackened and he stopped turning over and things started to fall on his head, first with a thump, thump, thump, then with a ping, ping, ping. He put his paw up to feel the top of his head and found that it was coated with ice; then his shoulders started to ice up, then his back and chest and soon he was a gleaming silver bear, ice-armoured all over. He was growing heavier and heavier and before long he had stopped going up and was hanging suspended five miles above the earth, a refrigerated cub at the top of a thunder cloud, as stiff as a poker and completely dumbfounded.

Then down he started to sink through the miles of swirling cloud until he nearly reached the bottom again, and the ice began to melt off him and he was able to take a few gasping puffs of breath before the up-draught seized him and shot him upwards again on another journey, coating him with a second layer of ice. He seemed inescapably caught in the thundercloud and up and down he went, quite losing count of the number of his journeys, and up and down with him went his drum and the broken twigs and leaves and the drops of water imprisoned in the cloud, and all of them were coated with layer upon layer of ice, transparent, gleaming and hard.

How they all escaped it is difficult to tell, but the great menacing insatiable bulk suddenly changed its mood and with a careless dispersal of its skirts and a sulky grumble of thunder, it relieved itself of its icy prisoners and scattered them angrily over the earth in a violent hailstorm. Luckily for Hob he fell on his nose, or we should never have heard of him again, because by this time the ice had closed him right up and he was unable to breathe. But the impact of his fall cracked his nose open and he could take great glorious breaths of air and be thankful that that part of the adventure was over. But he was not able to move the rest of himself at all. He was encased in a hard coat of ice, layers and layers thick and very nearly unsmashable.

You would think that by now the weather had done quite enough to poor Hob, and probably as he had fallen on a hot dry plain, if he had been allowed to stay there for long enough, the sun would have melted his ice coat and he would have been able to go home. But he was not so lucky, because on this plain there lived a family of fierce dust-devils known as the willy-willies, wanton whirling savage creatures who as soon as the sun grew hot would race about, snatching up armfuls of dust and sand or anything else that they might find lying about, and spin away like crazy teetotums and deposit their loads at the entrance to a castle which stood in the middle of the plain. These dust-devils were the servants of a giant and his wife who lived in the castle and who were called Mucker and Mopus O'Mullock. The willy-willies were not very good servants, because they hardly ever did what they were told unless it suited them to do it. But it did suit them to pick things up and rush off with them and spin them round and round, and they were quite content to shoot them out in front of the castle, because a dust-devil does not want to possess things of its own and will never hold anything for long, but always wants to be tearing off looking for something new. All kinds of things were brought to O'Mullock's gate and he made his living this way, and the arrangement suited him very well. Occasionally he ordered the dust-devils to bring in something special, but generally he left it to chance, and every day he would put on his boots and come out through the castle gate to find out what had been

delivered; often there were only saucepans and perambu-
lator wheels and bones and quantities of dust, but every
now and then he picked up a real bargain like a diamond or
a gold nugget or a rich shopkeeper prepared to pay an
enormous ransom.

Hob had not been lying on the plain for long and his
ice coat had scarcely started to drip before one of the willy-
willies found him, picked him up and whirled him off
unceremoniously and deposited him under the castle walls,
and with him were deposited the drum and many of the
ice-covered oddments that had been with him inside the
thundercloud. So when O'Mullock went out to do his
muck-raking he was confronted with piles and piles of
enormous hailstones. He whistled. He had never seen
anything like this before and called his wife to come and
look.

'Did hever you see hanythink to beat hit, Mops?' he
exclaimed. 'Hand hall brought for nothink!'

'Lor' beggar my cats!' said Mopus. ''Ooder thought hit!'

The giant fetched a wheelbarrow and he started to load
up the hailstones and wheel them inside the castle yard. He
was delighted. This was just what he wanted to cool their
wine and keep their food fresh. There was a chute down to the
cellar in the yard, and as O'Mullock brought in the hailstones he pitched them down the chute into the cellar
below. He was in a hurry to get as much in as possible
before the sun melted it, so he did not spare much time to
examine what he was gathering. But he did look curiously
at Hob lying helpless like a fly in amber and remarked:
'Coo! Cub hin haspic!' before flinging him down the chute
with the rest.

You may have been wondering what Hob had been
feeling all this time but, truth to tell, he had had very little
time to feel anything except surprise. He was not a brave

cub and generally made a fuss at once if anything unusual
happened to him, but who could make a fuss at a thunder-
cloud or even at a dust-devil? And fussing at a giant when
he was lying imprisoned inside a block of ice would have
been out of the question. So, when he reached the bottom
of the cellar chute among all the other hailstones, instead
of fussing, he started to think of ways in which he could
help himself. First of all he badly needed more room. His
thick fur had trapped air in between himself and his ice
covering, so he was not as uncomfortable as a human being
would have been, as nowhere did the ice touch his skin.
He started to puff himself out and breathe deeply and made
as hot a patch all round his nose as he could, and soon he
found the ice was melting off his face and he could open and
shut his mouth. Then he wriggled his head and snapped
and coughed and blew until his eyes and ears were free and
the ice was starting to crack off round his neck. Then he
had to stop, because all this made a lot of noise and he
could hear the giants up above arguing over their house-
keeping.

'Stop tipping, you clinchpoop, or you'll lose hall the
gravy!'

'Gurr! Gravy hor no gravy, she's got to go, the beauty!'

'Don't slop, you hold sorcepinlid you! 'Ere, lemme 'old
hit!'

'Clam hup your mug, fusspot, hor keep your wind to
cool your pie, hif the hice 'asn't done hit for you!'

The first load of provisions was being lowered on to
the ice. Hob lay very still, but as soon as the giants had left
to fetch some more, he started again on his efforts to free
himself. Luckily for him the lid was off the shute and the
sun shone directly down into the cellar. He began to drip,
then his front paws broke free, and it was not long before
he was able to struggle out of the rest of his ice coat and

creep away into a corner of the cellar, where he could dry himself out and watch the rest of the operations in safety.

The giants went on lowering food and drink into the cellar until it was too dark for them to see. There were bottles of wine and pies and sausages and hams and baskets of apples and huge pink melons and cottage loaves and jars of honey and jars of jam. Hob's mouth watered and his eyes nearly popped out of his head. He was a prisoner, it is true, but never had a prisoner had such a wonderful array of things to eat. He could hardly wait until the giants had finished for the day, replaced the lid on the chute and clumped away.

But after a few days Hob was surfeited with food. He had been very greedy and had made himself ill and then he did not have the sense to stop eating. Now he was overfed, depressed, afraid and very lonely. He searched about among the hailstones and found his drum. He cracked the ice off it and was a little comforted by something familiar, but he did not dare to beat it for fear the giants should hear. He became so miserable and bored that he had almost made up his mind to give himself up and take the consequences, when one evening he heard something—rather faint and muffled but quite distinct. Bursting with excitement he seized his drum and beat out a long, bold, 'Rat a tat-tat! Rat a tat-tat! Rat a tat-tat!'

Cob and Nob and Tob were feeling very guilty. Hob and his drum had annoyed them so much that they had driven him away by chanting at him, 'Go away, Hob! Go away, Hob!' until he really had gone away and had never come back. It was more than two weeks ago that they had last seen him marching off rather indignantly with his drum into the forest. That was on the day of the big hailstorm which had stripped the leaves off the trees and pitted the half-ripe apples so that now they looked as though they had all had smallpox. Nob was terribly afraid that Hob had been killed in the storm and every day she searched apprehensively, fearing lest she should come upon his poor furry body lying under a tree root. Cob thought that he had just got lost because he was always so stupid about finding his way. He did not expect to find Hob's body, but he did think he might find some footprints or some sign which might tell him in what direction Hob had gone. He did trace him as far as the little grassy hill, but after that there was nothing, and soon his own footprints were everywhere but there were no more of Hob's.

Tob sat at home and thought. He was convinced that if Hob had got lost he would have got lost immediately only a few yards from the den, and then he would have sat down and beaten his drum frantically until somebody had come to rescue him. So, he argued to himself, obviously he was not lost. And he was certain that if Hob had been killed in the storm somebody would have found his body by now. There were not only Cob and Nob searching for him but Thunder and Skyboy and Littleflame as well. No, Tob was certain that some person or animal or thing had carried Hob away and that if he was going to be found at all, it would be somewhere quite a long way off. He had once heard a story about a king who had been captured by his enemies and shut up in the tower of a castle. A faithful friend had set out to find him and every time he had come to a castle he had sung some old familiar song underneath the windows. After travelling half across the world and singing under hundreds of castle towers he had reached one where his song had been answered from inside. So he knew that he had found the king and somehow he had rescued him, but Tob could not remember that part of the story. He felt sure, though, that this was the way to find Hob. So when he had quite made up his mind, he consulted Cob and Nob.

'Us doesn't know no castles,' objected Cob.

'Our Mam wouldn't never let us,' objected Nob.

'Our Mam's that cut up she won't never care,' answered Tob, 'an' if they done be castles us done be find them.'

So the long and the short of it was that Cob, Nob and Tob decided to set off together to find Hob, and because Hob was not very good at singing by himself like the king in the story and might not be able to answer them, they got Skyboy to make another drum like the one he had made for Hob. They told Mother Bear what they were going to do, and she was so unhappy at the loss of Hob that she did not try to stop them going, only told them to be careful, not to be away for too long and not to scold Hob when they found him.

It was a sad sight to see the three young bears set off on their quest. They had all been searching for Hob for so long already that deep down inside themselves they had given up hope, so they started off tired and dispirited, dragging along in single file, Cob trailing the drum, Nob carrying her new spindle and Tob clutching a small bundle of food which had been given them by their mother.

''Tis like us won't never get nowhere!' sighed Tob despondently to himself, then remembering how boldness and resource had helped him through some awkward situations in his adventure with the goblins, he took the drum from Cob and stepped out in front beating a smart marching tattoo. Their spirits rose immediately and they drummed themselves along through the forest, taking turns at the drumming and keeping it as brisk and cheerful as they could.

But in the first three days the only dwelling places that they found were an owl's hole in a willow tree, a rabbit's hole in a bank and a mole's castle in the middle of the road. And when they drummed outside the owl's hole he glared down at them with his huge terrifying golden eyes, and when they drummed outside the rabbit's hole the rabbit came out and chattered its teeth, more like a rat than a rabbit, and the mole did nothing at all except heave a little more earth from down below on to the top of his castle.

On the fourth day they came to the end of the forest. It stopped quite suddenly, and they were able to sit on the edge of it and dangle their feet into a treeless plain, like people who had unexpectedly reached an ocean and had started to paddle. The plain was dull, flat, dusty and wide. The day was hot and they looked at it with distaste, not wishing to leave the shady trees and launch out into such a glaring waste. A dusty haze made it impossible to see how far it was across to the other side, if indeed there was another side.

They decided to go no farther that day, but had very little spirit left to make a camp. They poked about among the tree roots to find a little food or curled up under the bushes to doze. In the heat of the afternoon the plain became dotted with dust-devils pirouetting over the bare ground like dervishes, picking up armfuls of dust, swirling them round, then dropping them and disappearing. These greatly interested Tob, who watched their aimless play for a long time. If only one could persuade a dust-devil to pick up what one wanted it to pick up, he thought, and then put it down again where one wanted it put down, it might be made into a very useful kind of creature. He gathered up some leaves and twigs and carried them out a few yards on to the plain and put them in a little heap, hoping to tempt one of the devils into picking them up. As he was leaning down to place them, along came a devil out of nowhere, whirled the leaves into the air, spun Tob round violently once or twice and dashed off, leaving him flat on his back. He retreated quickly among the trees and decided that they were not friendly creatures. As the day grew cooler the dust-devils disappeared and at sunset there were none of them left at all, but something else came into sight which made the tired cubs crane their necks and stare while their jaded spirits went up by leaps and bounds.

One after another the towers and windows of an imposing castle, standing out in the middle of the plain, started to shine and glitter in the light of the sinking sun. The dust had hidden them in the afternoon but before the sun had disappeared the whole castle had come clearly into view and after dark lighted windows in the towers still showed clearly where it stood. On their journey the bears had been discouraged by finding no houses or castles where they could beat their drum—they hardly counted the homes belonging to the owl, the rabbit and the mole—and however good the drum-beating idea was, it was no use at all if there was nowhere to do the beating. But now in front of them was a splendid-looking place with lots of towers and windows and, as far as they could tell, nothing at all to stop them sitting down outside and beating to their hearts' content. And doing something was better than doing nothing, even if there was no answering beat from inside. They felt quite excited when they cuddled down together to go to sleep, although Tob did have one or two uncomfortable doubts about the dust-devils.

Next morning was fine and bright. The castle was standing out clearly against the light, and there were no dust-devils in sight. The cubs did not even stop to find breakfast but marched straight out on to the plain with Cob leading, beating the drum.

It was a terribly long way to the castle. The distance had been quite deceptive in the brightness of morning and they marched and they marched, and they beat on their little drum and they marched some more, and the sun got hotter and hotter, and still the castle seemed to be miles away. Then up got the willy-willies, who were late risers but none the less vicious for that, first a little one at their feet which whisked away with a handful of sand, then a bigger one behind them which raced by with a cunning tweak at the drum, tearing it out of Cob's paw and bowling it off in front of them, so that they all raced to catch up with it and fell on it helter-skelter, tumbling on top of each other, quite unprepared for a third dust-devil which spun by over the top of them, filling their eyes with sand and knocking them all flat just as they were getting back on to their feet.

'Hold our paws!' shouted Cob desperately, but he was too late. He and Tob and the drum managed to stay together, but Nob and her spindle were torn away rotating like a top right in the middle of a towering willy-willy, and her horrified brothers watched her skimming over the plain towards the castle at sixty miles an hour. Cob set up a great roar of anger and started to race after her, but before he could close his mouth it was filled with sand and pebbles as another devil struck them from behind. Tob clung to him desperately and they emerged from the struggle coughing and choking and shaking the dust out of their eyes and their ears. Tob, who generally looked so mildly out of his bespectacled eyes, suddenly began to get angry. He had had every funny bone in his body mercilessly battered. He picked up a stick which had been dropped by a careless dust-devil and brandished it above his head.

'One more o' thee scruffety ole devils do come near I . . .' he threatened, but got no further, because a real scruffety devil whipped up in front of him and started to buzz him like a humming-top. But it had reckoned without Tob's temper, and although he felt as though the fur was being blown off

his skin he managed to give three tremendous blows on to the ground under the dust-devil, and lo and behold! the devil was no more, it disintegrated like a bubble and nothing was left but a small heap of sand and a very rumpled and giddy Tob.

He was not at all sure whether the dust-devil had disappeared by chance in the rather pointless way they had or whether it had gone by virtue of his three great blows on the ground. He looked round and found Cob still intact, humped in a protective huddle nearby. He picked up another stick and pushed it at him.

'Do'ee swipe three great swipes down into his innards!' he urged desperately, and hardly had he said it when he was again swiping madly at another attacker which came roaring across at them as though to avenge its companion. Down it went like the last one, and they were left gaping at empty space and another pile of dust.

Now began the incredibly slow and difficult advance of Cob and Tob towards the castle. Cob tied the drum securely round his neck to free his front paws. They clung to each other tightly, sticks in their free paws, keeping a look out in front, behind and at the sides for the attacking willy-willies. Having seen two of their companions defeated, the dust-devils were a little more cautious, but they came on at such a speed and jinked and veered so unpredictably that the bears were involved time and again in violent swiping battles before they managed to reach the walls of the castle. And now the day was drawing towards evening and most of the devils had disappeared. Cob and Tob threw themselves down with relief and lay for a while recovering their breath before starting on their next task, which was to find Nob.

It did not take them long to find her although they walked past her several times without recognizing her.

While winding her up inside itself the willy-willy had unwound her spindle and wrapped her up in the wool so that she looked like a caterpillar's cocoon. Tob and Cob stood her upright and took it in turns walking round and round unwinding her and winding the wool back on to the spindle. She was not badly hurt but very giddy and confused, so they sat her down between them until she felt better.

All around was a strange collection of debris, all the things that the dust-devils had picked up in their dizzy journeys that day and thrown against the castle walls. There was a lot of dust and sand, but sticking up among the dust and sand were old umbrellas, teapots and shoes and rags and, luckily for the cubs, quite a scattering of potatoes. They collected these and ate them hungrily, as they had not had any food so far that day. They were worn out, and Cob and Tob felt that it would have been much easier if they had allowed themselves to be carried in by the willy-willies, which would have saved all that walking and fighting. Nob did not agree. She said that a journey inside a dust-devil was worse than being chased by Ollafubs and that the worst part of it was being thrown out at the end. She had a big swollen egg on her head where she had been banged against the castle wall.

They could hear footsteps and voices inside the castle, so they decided to do no drumming until after dark. They lay resting and listening and discussing in whispers, wondering who could be living inside a castle which looked so grand, but which had such a terrible rubbish heap at its front gate. Lights soon shone in some of the windows and shutters were pulled to and bolted. They heard a gust of very raucous laughter and shivered. They were really feeling very nervous.

When it was quite dark and most of the lights in the

windows had gone out and there were no more noises inside the castle, they plucked up all their courage and started to drum, very, very softly at first and then, when nothing happened, a little louder and a little louder.

'Sh!' said Nob suddenly. They stopped drumming and listened. What was it? Nothing at all. They drummed again. 'Sh!' she said again. Surely from somewhere underneath another drum was answering. They drummed again much louder. Now it was unmistakable, a real martial tattoo from right underneath their feet. 'Rat a tat-tat! Rat a tat-tat!'

They were so excited they threw caution to the winds and beat out the loudest roll they could on their drum, 'Rat a tat-tat! Rat a tat-tat! Rat a tat-tat!' and from underneath came an answering roll just as loud, 'Rat a tat-tat! Rat a tat-tat! Rat a tat-tat!'

'How come he do be down under?' asked Nob wonderingly. They had certainly all expected Hob to be up in a tower like the king, but neither Cob nor Tob seemed to think that this was important. Their plan had worked, they had discovered Hob and now they really let themselves go and beat the drum for all they were worth, and from underneath came just as loud a banging, because Hob was just as pleased and excited as they were.

But what about Mucker and Mopus O'Mullock, the master and mistress of the castle? They had gone to bed; they were just getting off to sleep when the drumming started. At first they tried to shut it out by pulling the bedclothes over their heads, but then it became so loud that they just could not stand it. Mucker leaped out of bed and dashed to the window and pushed back the shutters. He could see nothing, but he could hear a lot and he could guess pretty well from where the sound was coming. He stretched an immensely long arm out of the window and scooped all three cubs and their drum into his enormous hand, drew them up through the window and banged the shutter to behind them. Now all four cubs were inside the castle.

All that sleepy O'Mullock wanted to do was to get back to bed as quickly as possible, so without even glancing at what he had picked up, he jammed them into the boot cupboard and slammed the door. The cupboard was pitch dark and full of huge obstacles. The cubs hardly dared to move and spent a very uncomfortable sleepless night. However were they going to help Hob now that they were all prisoners too?

The giant forgot all about them until after breakfast, when it was his custom to go to his boot cupboard and get out a pair of boots to put on before going outside the gate to find what the dust-devils had brought him. When he opened the cupboard he saw the three cubs sitting inside, looking dreadfully frightened and unhappy.

'Twist me pink hand some!' he exclaimed. 'So you was the little demons making hall that row! Hand keeping me from my righteous rest! Come hout hand let me look hat you!'

He pulled the cubs out one by one and sat them on the table in a row. He sat down in front of them and stared at them, then he shouted to his wife:—

''Ere, Mops dearie! See what hi've found!'

Mopus came in. She was a large stout giantess and wore a frilled cap which made her face look like a vast pastry tart. She stared at the cubs too.

'Jigger me green!' she said after a while. ''Owhever hin the world did they get 'ere?'

Both giants scratched their heads and stared some more, then—'Hi've got hit!' shouted O'Mullock so loud that he nearly blew the cubs off the table. 'Hall halong hof the hice hand the 'ailstones! Hi chucked one down that was like ha hegg hin haspic hand 'ere's the rest!' He went off into a roar of laughter and banged his fist on the table so that the young bears bounced up and down alarmingly.

'Well, there hain't ha clink hof money to be got from them!' said Mopus, shaking her head. 'We'll put them to work, hand then we'll see!'

So that is what happened. The cubs were set to work without any breakfast. Tob was given a bucket and mop and told to scrub a passage which looked to him at least a mile long. Cob was given an enormous broom and told to sweep the yard and Nob was given a potato peeler and put at the kitchen sink. She thought it dreadfully hard to manage and when Mopus was not looking, nibbled off the potato skin with her front teeth. They all three worked very hard and at the end of the day were given a wretched dish of turnips between them for supper.

Life in the giants' castle revolved round potato peeling, sweeping, scrubbing, sauce-pan scouring and polishing boots, and a dull dispiriting life it was, with not even a square meal to look forward to. The giants were not unkind, but they were alarming and very mean. They could not bear potatoes to be peeled thickly, they hoarded every crumb from their own table and put it back into the larder, they provided no soap or hot water, and were always taking things out of cupboards and counting them and putting them back again. But what worried the cubs far more than all this was that they could find no further trace of Hob. They were convinced that it had been Hob drumming, but wherever was he?

Cob had often noticed a heavy cover over a hole in the yard when he had been sweeping. He had thought nothing of it until one day, when he was rattling the handles with the broom, Mopus shouted out angrily at him to stop and never to interfere with the cover again. Of course Cob started to wonder why the cover should be so important, so one day when Mopus was safely in the kitchen teaching Nob to knead bread (a job which Nob liked because she could suck her paws), he carefully lifted it a little way and pushed it to one side. He peered down on to a sloping chute running down into a cellar. He could see very little, but he said 'Woof!' into the hole and was very startled to hear 'Woof!' coming out of the hole. He stared into the darkness and saw two eyes staring back.

''Tisn't never our Hob!' he exclaimed in amazement.

''Tis true, 'tis I,' answered Hob. 'I done think you done been an' gone away again.'

'Pears an' ruddy apples!' exclaimed Cob. 'Kin you git up?'

''Tis too slopey,' said Hob. 'Git I a rope an' I kin.'

Just then Cob heard Mopus's heavy steps and he hurriedly replaced the lid and went on sweeping. But he was brimming with excitement and as soon as work was over he whispered his discovery to Tob and Nob. They were immensely happy that Hob was safe, but puzzled as to what they should do. Instead of having to get one bear out of the castle they now had to get four. But the first thing to do was to talk to Hob again, and when they next got an opportunity, the whispered conversation down the chute brought one good piece of news. There was plenty to eat down there. Any plan was greatly influenced by this fact. The three cubs upstairs were starving and Hob was dreadfully overfed. So they decided that Hob should be brought up somehow and the others let down in turn and as long as there were always three cubs to do the work, the giants were unlikely to notice which three cubs were doing it.

The problem now was how to get Hob up, and here Nob's woollen yarn on her spindle came into its own. She only had to double and twist it two or three times before it was strong enough to hold a small bear. Then they had to choose which one of them should go down first. Nob, whose work in the kitchen gave her opportunities for licks and surreptitious snacks, was not quite so hungry as Cob and Tob, so she agreed to go last. Cob and Tob drew lots and the lot fell to Tob.

Then it was necessary to occupy Mopus and keep her out of the way—O'Mullock was generally busy muck-raking and would stay away for hours. Nob suggested to Mopus that the sugar lumps were disappearing too fast, and once the suspicion was in her mind she would hardly leave the kitchen, but spilled the sugar lumps out on to the table behind closed curtains and doors and counted them over and over again. This gave the bears their opportunity and with Nob in the passage keeping guard, Cob and Tob opened the chute lid, let down the woollen rope and hauled up Hob.

There was a lot of delighted hugging and kissing in the yard, and then Tob was put on to the end of the rope and lowered down the chute and the lid fixed back firmly into its place. Hob was quickly instructed how to use a brush and pail and when Mopus had finished counting her sugar lumps and locked them back into the cupboard, and had drawn the curtains and opened the door, and when O'Mullock had finished searching among the rubbish piles, they found everything in order, with three cubs working diligently at the jobs to which they had been allotted.

Tob did not spend all his time eating when he was in the cellar. He broke off a monstrous piece of apple pie and took a hunk of bread and honey which was as big as a doorstep, and, with the pie in one paw and the bread and honey in the other, he started to explore the cellar, taking alternate bites as he went. It was not completely dark as there were ventilation holes and cracks in the ceiling, and when his eyes got used to the dimness, he found he could see a good deal. There was a stone staircase leading down from a door which was locked, and the walls were of stone, but in places damp had oozed through from outside, and the stones were loose. This was more particularly the case on what he guessed must be the outer wall of the cellar.

''Tis us bears as kin dig,' he said to himself with his mouth full, and tried shifting a stone. The first one was troublesome to move, but as soon as that was done he had no difficulty in enlarging the hole, and soon he had an opening large enough for a cub to creep into. But, of course, he was right underground and there was a lot of earth to tunnel through before he could reach the upper air. He went back for more pie and more bread and honey and then started to dig in earnest, and when it was time for Cob to be let down into the cellar and Tob to be pulled out, he had made a hole several yards long and, guessing that he was now clear of the castle wall, he had started to dig upwards on an incline. He had been greatly puzzled as to what to do with all the loose earth from the hole, because if either of the giants had visited the cellar and found piles of it lying about, they would have soon guessed that something strange was going on. After much thought he had pushed it all over to the base of the chute and stowed it neatly under the cakes and pies. He hoped that the pile of earth would grow at about the same pace as the pies and cakes diminished, but he doubted that even a bear could eat as much in a day as he could dig.

He passed his plan on hastily to Cob as they changed places and then told Hob and Nob. It was a good plan, and the hole grew and grew, but there was awful trouble in the kitchen when Hob took Nob's place, and if Mopus had not been as stupid as the pastry pie she so much resembled she would have guessed that something was wrong somewhere. Instead of which, when Hob could not manage the potato peeler at all, and when he dropped the tureen when she was dishing up the soup, all she did was to call him a great stupid girl, clumsy enough to have been a boy. He felt this to be such an insult, especially as he dared not refute it, that he burst into tears.

'You great gooby you!' exclaimed Mopus angrily, poking him in the ribs. 'Why, you're that fat! 'Alf rations for you, my girl, hand less than that hif you go hon so clumsy!'

The spectacle rings round Tob's eyes were 'dirt' to Mopus. She took the dish cloth and rubbed, then she took the scrubbing brush and scrubbed, complaining crossly that if 'she' could be clean one day there was no reason for 'her' to be dirty another day. Both Hob and Tob hated the kitchen and were thankful that their turns did not come very often.

Then one day something dreadful happened. O'Mullock decided to visit his cellar and see how his supplies of food and wine were keeping. Tob was down below and had been having some trouble with the walls of the tunnel, which in one place kept falling inwards. He had thought of a successful way to stop this happening and he was now busy riveting the sides with hard biscuits, of which there were plenty in the giant's store. He was taken by surprise. There were biscuits lying about, some of them broken, and, what is more, there was a pie exposed with a large piece bitten out of the top. He heard O'Mullock unlocking the door and bolted into the hole in a panic, pulling as many stones after him as he could to hide the entrance. The giant stamped heavily down the staircase and swung his lantern to and fro. The first thing he saw was the broken biscuits.

'Rats!' he growled, ''aven't 'alf been hat the grub! Hi'll 'larn 'em!'

He clumped round the cellar and stopped suspiciously at

the hole and kicked out the loose stones with the toe of his boot. Tob held his breath and shivered.

'Some rats!' said O'Mullock, evidently impressed by the size of the hole.

He went back up the cellar staircase, but Tob did not hear the door close, so he stayed in the hole and listened. Presently O'Mullock returned with a big rat trap, which he baited with cheese and set in the middle of the cellar. He then went away grumbling and turned the key in the door. Tob crept out of the hole and stepped gingerly all round the trap. The cheese smelled very good, but the metal smelled dangerous. He took one of the pink melons and lobbed it on to the trap. There was a sharp 'Snap!' a bit of the melon flew off and the trap jumped across the floor. Tob took up the melon and examined it. It had a big gash on one side and the juice was dripping out. He lobbed it at the trap again, but this time nothing happened.

''Tis like 'twould of bit my paw,' he reflected. Then he rescued what remained of the melon and ate it. After testing the trap several more times he decided it was dead, so he ate the cheese and found that it was very good, and all that he had learned about the trap he passed on to the others, so although O'Mullock reset the trap every day, he always found it sprung and the cheese stolen. This made him very angry and he decided that he must fill in the hole.

That very day it was Cob's turn in the cellar. He was digging busily when suddenly he saw daylight ahead and pushed his nose out into the fresh air. The first thing he saw was O'Mullock's back bent over the rubbish heaps collecting suitable things with which he could stuff up the 'rat' hole. Cob withdrew his head quickly and pulled some rags and rubbish into the mouth of the hole to hide it. He was waiting anxiously at the bottom of the chute when the others came to pull him out and let down Nob in his place.

They decided at once that they must make their escape that very evening, and told Nob to wait for them inside the hole with a good supply of food and that they would join her as soon as the giants had gone to sleep.

Nob spent an agonizing day sitting as near as she dared to the top of the hole, clutching a big apple tart. She could hear O'Mullock stuffing things into the mouth of the hole and hammering them firm with the toe of his boot and she became nearly frantic with the thought that, although she herself was free, she was now separated by this barrier from her brothers. It was bad enough to be a captive but far worse to be alone. She even began to look back at the potato peeler with regret and felt that a small supper of turnips in company was better than all the lonely banquets in the world.

After an hour or two of hammering and banging O'Mullock felt that he had made a good job of the hole. He re-set the trap and looked at the food store by the light of the lantern. He did not like the look of it at all. The hailstones had nearly all melted and there seemed to be a great deal of mud about. The food was beginning to look decidedly stale and he almost thought fly-blown, if there had been any flies in the cellar, which he knew there were not. He was cross and suspicious. He certainly did not want the job of carrying everything upstairs again and yet there seemed to be something going very wrong with his admirable arrangements. Perhaps there was an enemy about as well as rats. He would have to look to his possessions. He clumped up the stairs again feeling very put out.

The giants generally went to bed as soon as it was dark because they were mean about lights and could not bear to burn them unnecessarily. But that night they fell out over the matter of rats eating their provisions and hailstones not staying frozen for ever. They quarrelled noisily for a time and called each other awful names, then they made up their quarrel and their reconciliation was followed by a kind of miserly frenzy in which they decided to sit up in their bed-room all night and count their money. So they filled up their oil lamp, drew two chairs up to the table and spilled all the money out of their money bags and started to count.

Unfortunately the cubs still slept in the boot cupboard which was inside the giants' bedroom, and the door of the boot cupboard creaked. It was quite impossible for them to escape while the giants were still awake, and they crouched there in the dark suffering the same agonies of anxiety that Nob was suffering in the hole.

It seemed to Nob that she had been waiting for hours and hours since darkness fell. She had expected to hear the others pushing and scratching at the other side of the giants' barrier, but she heard nothing. She crept back down the hole to listen and banged into a saucepan handle in the dark. The blow hurt and shook her out of her paralysis of fear which had made her unable to do anything but sit and clutch her tart.

'Gin that be what he done bung her with, 'tis Nob'll un-bung her!' she said fiercely and started to pull and push the rattletrap arrangement of tins and lids and old bits of junk. O'Mullock was a poor workman, and although the stopping of the hole looked formidable enough, actually everything was rattly and loose and before long Nob had pushed her way through and cleared the hole. Action made her feel much better. She sniffed around the cellar and helped herself to a cake which she carried up the hole and put beside her tart. She poked her head out into the air and looked at the stars which seemed so inviting and free, and she wondered whether Mother and Father Bear were looking at them too. She thought she could smell the dawn and her anxiety returned. If they did not escape tonight, the giants could not fail to discover their plan with all that mess in the cellar and the tins and lids lying about. In desperation, she crept out of the hole and along under the castle wall until she was right underneath the giants' window. She saw the light, and she heard the coins clinking down one by one as the giants built their money piles, and she heard O'Mullock's voice counting and Mopus joining in at the dozens. Nob had never seen them counting money, but the counting of sugar lumps was fresh in her mind and she guessed what was happening.

"'Tis them skinny ole screws a-countin' an' a-countin'," she muttered in disgust to herself, and without thinking what she was doing she picked up a pebble and pitched it straight through the window and then turned round and bolted for the hole. The pebble landed on the table, scattering a pile of coins, then bounced against the lamp, shattering the glass chimney in pieces. The flame leaped and hissed and both giants rushed to the window. Cob, Tob and Hob in the cupboard heard the disturbance and deciding it was now or never for their escape, pushed open the creaky door and raced helter-skelter down the passage. O'Mullock was shouting threats into the dark and Mopus was scrabbling for the scattered coins, and neither of them gave a thought to the cubs or had any idea that they were gone.

The bears scurried across the yard, opened the chute and slid down into the darkness. They could not replace the lid, so they knew that the giants would soon discover their way of escape, so speed was everything. They each snatched some food as they passed through the cellar, and then scrambled as fast as they could through all the tins and saucepan lids up the escape hole and out into the open air.

But where was Nob? In her alarm she had lost the hole and was galloping frantically up and down trying to find it, banging into tins, rattling old bedsteads and generally making a terrible noise. Certainly she was not difficult to find, no more difficult than an elephant in an ironmonger's. But now the giants were thoroughly aroused and all hopes of a secret escape with many quiet hours of darkness before them had quite disappeared. They caught Nob and shook her to bring her back to her senses, then set off as fast as they dared, remembering the long distance to be travelled over the dusty plain.

It was already getting light and unfortunately it was going to be hot, and the hotter it was the more the willy-willies liked it. But they were still in bed, and the giants were still running round investigating the noise and stowing away their money. But it did not take them long to guess what had happened because of the empty boot cupboard and the open chute in the yard. They went down into the cellar by the stairs and saw the re-opened hole, the lids and tins lying about and a clear bear's footprint across the top of a jam tart. O'Mullock stood at the 'rat' hole and swore and Mopus sat beside the ruined provisions and wept.

'Hif hi'd hof known, hi'd hof hate them myself!' was all she could say, but it was not clear whether she was referring to the bears or the pies. O'Mullock had no intention of chasing after the bears himself. He knew a far better way of catching them or anyway he thought he did. First of all, he went and put on his boots. He was in no hurry at all. It was still morning and there was plenty of time. Then he strolled outside the castle gate and whistled up the willy-willies. It was such a fine, hot, sunny day that they were feeling most obliging. They whisked round him bowing and pirouetting, ready to do anything he wanted.

'Those three bears!' ordered O'Mullock grimly. 'Catch them! Spin them till their hinsides his their houtsides hand bring them 'ere!'

Their orders were clear enough and off went the dust-devils in great spirits ready for a good day's fun. But did you notice that O'Mullock made a mistake? He said 'three bears' and, of course, there were really four bears, but he had never found that out. So when the dust-devils caught up with the cubs about half-way across the plain, they carried out their orders and did snatch up three bears, but there was always a fourth bear with free paws and a stick to give those three tremendous swipes which broke up the dust-devils and made them drop their prey. It was a running battle between bear cubs and willy-willies, but in the end the bear cubs won. As he reached the edge of the forest and jumped to safety Tob brandished the pie that he had been struggling to hold all through their retreat and flung it furiously into the centre of the last pursuing dust-devil.

'Do'ee take that to the ole turmigints! 'Tis us as don't never want no more dirty ole pies!'

It would be dull to describe the rest of their journey home and their triumphant arrival back at the den, marching in with both drums beating. Happiest of all were Mother and Father Bear. They examined each cub carefully and when they had made sure that each one was whole and unharmed, they made arrangements for a feast. And because a bear's feast takes a very long time and is not the kind of feast that you would like at all, we will leave them to enjoy it by themselves, telling each other over and over again about what can happen if you are unlucky enough to be snatched up either by a dust-devil or by a thunder-cloud.

# The Wishes

The bear cubs were having a 'wishing day'. This was rather like having a birthday, but instead of happening only once a year, it happened whenever they felt like it. They only had to decide that today was a wishing day and then go off together to their special wishing place, where they would give each other presents and then wish. If the wishes came true they would generally tell each other, but they did not have to tell and sometimes they kept them quite secret and never told.

The wishing place was a grassy lawn at the top of an ancient landslide where the earth had slipped away from the bare rocks taking with it trees and bushes, and leaving an uneven scar on the side of the otherwise forested hill. But all that had happened so long ago that new grass had grown and the uprooted trees and bushes had sent out shoots from their fallen stems or new saplings had sprouted in their place. The bears had chosen the wishing place because of an oak whose toppled trunk and bare roots made a knotted circular doorway through which they must creep to reach

the wishing place. To pass through this doorway was part
of the ceremony, and to go in any other way was forbidden.

This wishing day the cubs had asked Skyboy and Littleflame to join them. They had shown them the way through
the wishing door, and now they were all sitting on the
grass on the farther side. It was late in the year and a bitter
wind was blowing, and water dripping from the rocks
above was already forming icicles which hung like spears
in the keen air. The presents were laid out on the ground
wrapped in leaves and grass. The cubs liked the excitement
of guessing before they opened them.

''Tis main cold,' said Cob. 'Light us a fire, do'ee now. '

To the cubs a fire was the greatest of treats, most suitable
for a wishing day. They could never tire of gazing at it or
cease to wonder at its antics or its warmth or its ceaseless
appetite.

''Tis more shrammed nor us bears,' said Nob, flinging on
sticks from a safe distance.

'Let's make torches,' said Skyboy, who had dragged in
the top of a dead pine. He broke off branches and held
them in the flames, then whirled them round his head. The
bears held each other's paws and watched in pop-eyed
wonder.

''Tis like 'twere girt whirley flowers,' said Nob.

'Or sunsets,' said Cob.

Littleflame hugged her knees to keep herself warm, and
thought of her wish. She hoped that the others would finish
playing and get on with the wishing, it was so very cold.

'You wish first,' she said to Cob, 'then when we've all
wished we'll open the presents.'

The bears sat down solemnly and closed their eyes. They
were all wishing together, their furry faces screwed up in
the intensity of their wishes. Tob opened his eyes first and
did a little hopping dance around the fire.

''Tis Tob'll be the firstest ever!' he said excitedly.

'The firstest what?' asked Littleflame, but he merely danced some more and looked mysterious.

Cob took a pine branch and poked it gingerly into the flames.

''Tis Cob as do have to learn hisself,' he said and with great determination lifted it out and held it for a moment above his head before flinging it with relief into the fire.

Littleflame had wished, but Skyboy would not answer. He was staring into the red-hot middle of the fire and had gone into one of his absent silent moods, and the others knew that it was no good expecting him to speak. Nob had finished, so Hob asked anxiously:

'Kin us open up the presents?'

Each of them had brought one present, so it was really nothing but an exchange. They shut their eyes and picked. Hob gave a great shout.

'If it isn't never just what I done wish for!' he cried excitedly, holding up a honeycake in his paw. He had picked on Littleflame's contribution to the pile, perhaps he had even guessed that it was there before he did his wishing. There was a pine cone, an apple, a newly polished tosser, a feather from a peacock's tail, a shell and Hob's cake. Everybody seemed pleased and Littleflame brought another cake from under her tunic and divided it into six pieces. They sat nibbling their portions and staring into the fire.

'What was that?' Skyboy jumped up suddenly and listened. They all stopped eating and listened too, then, with their mouths still full and staring at each other uncomprehendingly, they felt the earth underneath them shudder, and the shudder ran up their bodies as though they had been sitting on the palm of a giant's hand and the giant had suddenly been struck with palsy. The cliff above them started to move, hurtling down rocks which tore long searing gaps through the trees, bounding in great leaps down the hillside. There was no cover except for the wishing door, and they scrambled for it, crowding underneath as a huge ice-covered slab cracked off and fell flat across the fire and the green grass on which they had been sitting. Two slender pine trees bent over and touched their heads upon the earth, then gravely righted themselves while a ripple like a sea-wave passed across the ground and disappeared.

''Tisn't never like what it did oughter be,' observed Tob, gravely shaking his head.

Now it was quiet and they crept out from under the wishing door and hurried down in single file through the trees, urged on by Skyboy who said that they must get away from under the cliff in case there was another quake which would dislodge another fall of rocks. They came to a turn in the path which should have given them a view of the village down below them in the valley. But the path just came to an end; there was nothing in front of them but a great drop into nothingness and a column of dust going up like smoke from a great fire. They looked at the dust and they looked at each other and then Cob sat down with a groan and held his head in his paws.

'I done wish too hard!' he said miserably.

'Whatever did you wish for, Cob?' asked Littleflame, aghast.

'I done wish for something as'd learn I to be brave.'

They stood looking out over the void and pondering the awful consequences of Cob's wish.

''Tisn't never like that,' said Tob wisely, shaking his head after a long unhappy silence. ''Twould of shook, whether or no. 'Tisn't never our Cob as done it.'

Cob looked at him gratefully, immensely relieved at his judgment.

''Tweren't never a earthquake as I done wish for,' he said.

'Well, it looks as though we'll all have to learn to be brave now,' said Littleflame. 'There just doesn't seem to be any way left of getting back home.'

They scrambled along the edge of the precipice, trying to find some familiar landmark or some way in which they could climb down and reach the village, but the earth seemed to have been split as though sliced by a hatchet, and the half that they were on seemed to be hopelessly divided from the half to which they wanted to go. Before dark the bears scratched out a hollow in the ground and they all dug in bear fashion, covering themselves as best they could with earth and leaves against the cold. When they woke the ground was white with frost and they were stiff and famished. Hob could hardly be persuaded out of the hole and he dragged wretchedly after the others, whimpering and rubbing his eyes, and then because he was not looking where he was going he tripped over a fallen branch and before anyone realized what was happening he had pitched headlong over the precipice. Littleflame had heard him stumble and looked round, she gave a cry of anguish and ran to the edge and gazed after him in agony as he bounced twice on the rocks and then spreadeagled across the branches of a thorn tree which had been uprooted and then caught up again on a jagged piece of the cliff.

'Hob!' she cried wildly. 'Hob! Are you alive? Are you all right? Hob!'

The others came running back and they all craned their necks to look over at poor Hob. Anybody else would have been killed, but there was a faint flutter from one of his paws.

''Tis like he do be live an' kicking,' said Tob.

'However are we going to get him up again?' cried Littleflame, tears streaming from her eyes.

Cob was too miserable to speak. Looking over the cliff

made his head swim and his stomach rise into his throat, and he could not get rid of the feeling that it was all his fault.

'We can't possibly climb down to him,' said Skyboy, 'and if we could, he couldn't possibly climb up. We shall have to make some sort of a rope.'

They set to work, but it took them until late afternoon, piecing together and twisting lengths of creeper, until they had a rope long and strong enough to reach Hob and to make fast to a tree and to tie around Hob's body at the other end. Cob's heart had been beating like a drum all the time that they had been at work, and his mouth had been getting drier and drier because he knew what he ought to do and he was going to do it.

'Let I!' he whispered hoarsely—he could barely speak. 'Let I, only do'ee shut up my eyes so as I don't never see nothing.'

Littleflame tied her cloth girdle over his eyes and they lowered him over the cliff, with Skyboy and Littleflame and Nob playing out the rope, and Tob shouting instructions from the edge. When Cob reached the thorn bush he put his paw out to feel Hob's fur and patted him encouragingly.

''Tis Cob,' he whispered. 'Bide still awhile. I do be going for to fix a rope for to pull 'ee up.'

Hob groaned. 'I'se that full o' spikeys 'tis like I were a teasel what's turned rightside in.'

The really difficult part of Cob's task was still to be done. He had to undo the rope which was round his own body and fix it firmly around Hob. He had to give the signal for Hob to be hauled up while he himself waited, clinging to the thorn bush until the rope could be let down for him. Then he would have to fix it again around himself—so far he could not even unbind his eyes—he was paralysed at the thought of all the difficult things he had to do. He could hear Skyboy's voice calling anxiously from above, and the urgency of the sound forced him at last to move. He pushed the cloth gingerly from his eyes and, willing himself neither to look up nor down, he deliberately freed himself from the rope, tied it firmly round Hob's middle, reinforcing it with the cloth girdle, and when all was ready, waved his paw, hoping that they would recognize this as the signal to pull. He saw the rope tighten and take Hob's weight and Hob's body gradually become airborne and disappear above his eye level. He dared not look up, his head started to spin, his insides seemed to surge up into his mouth and he caught sight of the ground below, and it started rushing up at him at a sickening pace. He shut his eyes tight before it reached him, and when the others looked over the edge ready to throw the rope down again, Cob had disappeared.

At first, no word was spoken by the unhappy company at the top of the cliff. There just seemed nothing to say. One cub had been rescued and another lost, and they all kept their thoughts to themselves. Hob seemed to have injuries, but he was so full of thorns and so cold from exposure that it was impossible to tell how seriously he was hurt. They carried him very gently away from the edge of the precipice and made him a bed in a sheltered hollow and covered him with moss.

'Cruddle 'ee down,' said Nob to comfort him. 'Us'll fetch up our Cob willy nilly.'

But when they went back to the place of the accident and let Skyboy down on the rope as far as the thorn bush he could see nothing at all below but the jagged teeth of rocks jutting from stony dark ground. They gave up hope, but Tob would not leave the place where Cob had gone over, but crouched there all night, staring dry-eyed into the darkness, mourning for his brother.

''Twas him as did learn hisself to be brave,' he thought over and over again.

Hob lay very still in his moss bed while they took it in

turns to sit by him. He was breathing steadily and he ate a little, so they felt that there was a good chance that he would get better. Meanwhile, they had to make the best of their chilly refuge, and bit by bit Littleflame extracted the thorns, which were mostly in his face and chest and stomach, as he had landed in the thorn bush face downwards. When the thorns were all out he seemed to get better, but although he could sit up, he still could not walk. It was growing more bitterly cold and Skyboy insisted that they must move down into the valley, so they set about making a stretcher on which they could carry Hob. This they did with two long poles and a hammock of plaited creepers in between. They padded it with moss and tied Hob on with more creepers. He groaned and grumbled, but it was a choice of freezing or going, and they did not take much notice of his complaints.

'Gin 'ee be peevish, 'ee kin bide lonesome,' said Nob to him firmly as they started off one chilly morning, and the threat of being left by himself silenced him.

Their progress was very slow. The earthquake had rumpled and churned the land so that many places were impassable, and often they had to retrace their steps or leave the stretcher with Hob on it hidden under bushes while they searched out a path. After weary days of journeying they reached more level ground and left the bitter hills behind them, and here to their surprise they found an old ruined house with part of its roof still on and enough walls standing to provide more shelter than they had seen since leaving home. Here they decided to stay until the weather grew warmer and Hob was well again.

They busied themselves repairing the roof, improvising a door to keep out the wind and collecting moss for beds and woodland foods to store. And they felt happier for having plenty to do. Skyboy tried hard to recognize their whereabouts, but the earthquake had so altered the landscape with great fissures and caverns and bowls of churned-up earth that his attempts were mere guesswork. And not more than a mile from the house was something he could not account for at all, a swift wide river which certainly had not been there before. To reach home again they would have to cross this river. Ice was now forming along its banks and every day more of the water was being covered, but there was still a dark forbidding stream down the middle which was as yet impassable.

With warmth and good food Hob began to recover fast. He was still convinced that he was lame, because of a notion firmly fixed in his head that somehow he had to balance Cob's loss which had happened on his account, by remaining disabled himself. So he would not even try to walk until one day Nob impatiently rolled him on to his four legs and told him to get on. To his surprise all his paws and all his legs worked. He was still not sure that this was right, so he developed a habit of shaking each paw in turn and then holding it up to his ear 'to see if she did rattle' as Nob put it. This irritated the others and they teased him so that he soon stopped doing it, and it was not long before he had forgotten all about his hurts and was skipping about as nimbly as ever he had done before.

About this time Nob took to disappearing sometimes for a whole day, and the small amount of food she brought home in the evenings hardly looked like the results of a day's search.

'Wherever have you been, Nob?' asked Littleflame after one of these long absences.

'I done been grubbin' aroun',' answered Nob evasively.

'Well, you haven't got much to show for it. A few roots and a mouthful of nuts—nobody would grow fat on that!'

''Tis like them mousies has ate it all.'

Nob's explanation was not very satisfactory, and one evening she returned with nothing at all, looking very dishevelled and tired Nobody questioned her, but they all looked at her disapprovingly and next day she asked Tob to go with her. She led him towards a rough fissured patch of ground where the earth had cracked and fallen in and the disruption had squeezed sharp fang-like rocks out of the ground, which were sticking up like teeth in the open mouth of a crocodile. As they drew near to this place Nob stopped and whispered to Tob to listen. Somewhere down below him he could hear moanings and floppings, as though a great soft body was rolling itself about. They crept forward and lay on their stomachs at the edge of a deep fissure and peered over. A tall strong pine had fallen into the crack and rocks had slipped across its trunk, and at the base of the tree something was moving and it was from here that the moans were coming. And if the moans had been words they would have been horrible cursing words, that was the kind of moaning that they heard. As Tob looked he could see one baleful eye glaring up at him out of the hole. He knew that eye, he had seen it before and could never forget it. He drew his head back from the edge and found that he was shaking all over.

''Tis a Ollafub,' he whispered. 'He done got stuck in that there hole.'

Then all his hair stood on end, because instead of finding Nob lying beside him, he saw that she was scrambling down the tree trunk towards the Ollafub; she was standing just above the tree roots and pitching things into the hole, pine cones, nuts and juicy roots. Tob could hear the Ollafub's jaws snapping and crunching as he caught the titbits and guzzled them up. When she had no more to throw, Nob scuttled back up the tree trunk and threw herself down beside him.

'He done pull hisself up lots gin I did start to feed him,' she said, shivering.

'Is you plain plum lunattic!' exclaimed Tob, looking at her with amazement. 'How come you be so dafty? Gin I kin do it, 'tis Tob'll fix him wi' a girt rock! 'Tis such he do ask for, not nuts an' sweeties an' such!'

''Tis you as don't never understand!' said Nob indignantly. ''Tis what I done wish for.'

Tob stared speechless at his sister. He was now sure that she was crazy.

'I done wish as I done find something as do be plum beastly an' hateful so's I kin be kind,' continued Nob. ''Tis like our Cob, I done wish too hard an' 'twere a Ollafub.'

Tob's conviction that Nob was mad changed slowly into reluctant admiration. He lay looking at her, trying to make up his mind whether her charity outweighed her lunacy or whether it was the other way round. And meanwhile down in his hole the Ollafub gnashed his teeth on the remaining nuts and thrashed around dangerously. Tob peered over the edge again, feeling quite nonplussed.

''Tis a middlin' dirty creature,' he remarked, looking at the Ollafub with distaste, and completely unable to think of anything else to say.

Now that she had introduced Tob to her private charity, Nob was willing to tell him how it had all come about. She wanted very much to be kind, but she found it too easy to be kind to somebody she liked, so she decided she must be kind to somebody she did not like—Mopus O'Mullock and her potato peeler had crossed her mind. With this in view, she had made her wish. But what an alarming shock it was to find that the wish had come so very true that it was an awful Ollafub that had to be the object of her kindness, an Ollafub pinned down in a hole by rocks and starving to death! The temptation to pretend to herself that she had not seen the Ollafub was almost too great for her, but then she remembered Cob learning to be brave to the last degree, and she was not going to be outdone. So feed the Ollafub she must, even though every day he was getting stronger and stronger and more and more able to pull himself out of his hole. And she felt that she must not only feed him, but reform him as well, teach him how to behave. She found to her satisfaction that he could understand her and she had struck a bargain with him. He had promised to be good and kind for ever if she would feed him and care for him until he was strong enough to get out of his hole. Poor unsuspecting kindly Nob!

They said nothing about the Ollafub to the others for some days, because they felt his presence such a problem that, beyond carrying out Nob's charitable resolve, they scarcely knew what to do. The more food they gave to the creature, the stronger he grew and the farther he was able to heave himself up and the more unpleasant he looked. Tob made up his mind that before he was free, he must have a bath, or he was going to refuse to help any more in this crazy arrangement. He had been studying the fallen tree trunk carefully and now had a bargaining point of his own. He could see that the only thing left that stopped the Ollafub from freeing himself altogether was a rock so placed that it could be levered up with comparative ease if enough weight could be put on the upper end of the tree. He thought that he and Nob together perched at the topmost point would probably do the trick. Whether it was a good thing to free the Ollafub at all hardly entered into it. The creature was growing so lusty and strong that he would free himself soon in any case. This was just bringing matters to a head more quickly, and cleaning up the Ollafub at the same time. So the next time they visited him, Tob put the suggestion to the Ollafub.

'What wi' floppin' aroun' in that there hole you done be main mucky an' dirty,' he said, holding his paw over his nose. The Ollafub showed his teeth and squinted at him.

''Tis me an' Nob'll fix you so as you done be free. But you did oughter be washed first.'

The Ollafub chattered angrily and lunged his head at him.

'Gin you done stay dirty an' vicious, us won't never fix you so as you done be free.' Tob spoke sternly and turned his back and moved away.

It took several days' persuasion and an illustration of how the freeing was to be done with Nob and Tob dangling half their weight at the top end of the tree, before the Ollafub would consent to his bath. Then what a prodigious undertaking it was, needing all their courage and strength to carry it through! They borrowed the wooden bucket which Skyboy had made for the house, they found two scrapy scratchy stones with which to pound and scrub the Ollafub in the same way as elephant keepers pound and scrub their elephants, they collected armfuls of gorse to use as hairbrushes and pine needles to use as tooth brushes and set off on their dangerous errand, wishing that it was any other job on earth that they were going to do.

The Ollafub was sulky and morose at first, and they scrubbed and pounded with a will, taking it in turns to do the washing and to hurry to and fro with fresh buckets of water and more stones and gorse, because everything was worn out almost immediately on that scaly spiky hide. Then the Ollafub grew angry and lashed out with his feet so that they had to scramble away up the tree trunk and threaten to leave him stuck for ever if he did not behave. But finally it was finished and he looked almost respectable, all except for his lower half, which was of course still stuck in the hole. They refused to free him that day—he spat and swore angrily—but said they would come back on the next day.

They first had to go home and warn the others of the rash thing that they had undertaken and of the unpredictable results of Nob's benevolence.

Skyboy and Littleflame were very grave and anxious when they heard about the Ollafub.

'You kind, stupid, crazy little bear!' exclaimed Skyboy. 'What a thing to do!'

'Us'll all be deaded same as Cob,' said Hob gloomily, and Littleflame thought that he was probably right. But in spite of this, they all agreed that Nob was right to stick to her side of the bargain whatever the consequences.

Next day Nob and Tob set off with much foreboding, carrying as much food as they were able, as they thought it would be safer to free the Ollafub after he had had a heavy meal. As they drew near the place their steps grew slower and slower and their hearts grew heavier and heavier. They sat down and nibbled at the food and they could hear the Ollafub slapping the rocks with his front hoofs and singing an awful kind of a song.

'Ole man moke wiv his bag of nuts, To ho To ho To ho!' He never seemed able to get beyond the first line, but sang that over and over again, and they could see the top of the fallen tree shaking violently.

''Tis like he do be fixin' hisself free,' said Tob anxiously. 'An' he won't never be thankin' us for fixin' him.'

''Tisn't no more use a-dawdlin' an' a-doodlin',' agreed Nob. 'Let us be a-goin' an' a-doin'.'

The Ollafub greeted them with an awful leer. He certainly had pulled himself up a great deal since his bath, and the water-mark between where he had been washed and where he had not been washed stood out clearly on his skin.

'Do'ee bide still awhile yet,' called Nob and bravely scrambled down the rocking tree trunk. She stood throwing nuts and pine-cones into his mouth, and between each mouthful she lectured the Ollafub severely on his promised behaviour on regaining his freedom. Tob stood above, looking on and wondering whether it was not a great mistake to imagine that boys were braver than girls.

'Me an' Tob done fetch you all this here grub, us done wash you clean an' respectable, 'tis you what's got to behave good an' mousy-like, an' don't 'ee never crackle your girt teeth nor roll your girt eyes nor flap your girt hoofs, never no more, see? Do'ee say aye, an' me an' Tob'll fix you free.'

The Ollafub shrugged his shoulders, crossed his front legs, lowered his eyelids and fixed an awesome grin on his face. This was his idea of looking civilized. Nob climbed slowly back up the tree trunk, not liking the look of him at all.

''Tis a powerful vicious body an' 'tis its hinderbits as do be powerful dirty,' she confided to Tob in a whisper as they started to scramble into the top branches of the tree. As their weight became effective and the base of the trunk began to rise there was a sudden loud pop like a cork coming out of a bottle. The Ollafub shot into the air with a bellow of triumph and landed with a great bump on the grass above the fissure in which he had been imprisoned.

Tob and Nob had hoped foolishly that they would be able to creep away, leaving the Ollafub to finish the food which they had left piled ostentatiously on the ground. But they were quite wrong. The Ollafub had gobbled the food before they could slip into the bushes and came galumphing after them. They zigzagged and circled, hoping that he might be sidetracked by something on the way, but in spite of everything they tried he was still following them closely when they arrived back at the house.

'Do'ee bide outside,' ordered Nob firmly, but the Ollafub had other ideas. He took hold of the door with his teeth and pulled it out; he pushed his way inside clumsily and lay down across all the beds. Their store of food was piled on a home-made table in the corner, conveniently within the Ollafub's reach. He lolled on the beds, helping himself idly to what he fancied. He was perhaps keeping his promise in that he was being reasonably quiet, neither flapping his hoofs nor rolling his eyes nor doing much crackling with his teeth, but it soon became obvious that their laboriously collected supply of food would have disappeared before the evening and that nobody would want to lie on those beds again. The children and cubs sat at a distance, shivering in the wind. Nob was devastated with remorse! This business of being kind was having formidable results.

Then she had an idea, not a very hopeful idea but one that was worth trying. Without saying anything to the others she got up and went towards the house, picked up the wooden bucket which was outside the door and rattled it angrily. The Ollafub looked out with his mouth crammed full.

'Do'ee stop a-grindin' an' a-guzzlin' or 'tis us as'll scrub 'ee tohind like us did scrub'ee tofore! 'Tis us as hasn't never had a bit nor a bite, ye girt greedy gobbler you!' Nob spoke with genuine fury, watching her well-earned supper sliding down into the creature's over-gorged stomach. The Ollafub poked out a long bluish-black tongue at her and then drew in his head. Nob took up a stick and beat the bucket fiercely. A few nuts and roots shot through the door, then the Ollafub turned round and sat himself down squarely in the entrance, using his own formidable back and behind to close it more securely than ever lock and key could have done. Nob brandished her stick and belaboured the exasperating posterior with all her strength, but the only reply was a switch of his rattlesnake tail.

Nob's reckless behaviour would certainly have led to

awful consequences had not Skyboy run up and seized her firmly and dragged her away in tears.

'Leave off, Nob!' he exclaimed angrily. 'You'll have us all eaten up if you go on like that! Ollafubs just don't know how to behave, and it's silly to think that you can teach them!'

'He done promise as he'd be good!' wailed Nob through her tears.

'Well, he is being good according to his ideas of being good. Can't you see? What's good to an Ollafub is just beastly and greedy and revolting to us and as long as he doesn't decide to change and be BAD, we've still got a chance.'

They held a quick consultation in whispers and decided that they must go at once while the Ollafub was still busy with the stores. It was a miserable decision to have to make; it was bitterly cold, it was nearly dark and they dared not even stop to rescue their small treasured possessions. Nob and Hob were in tears and the three others were on the verge of tears. The best that they could hope for was to find some sheltered hiding place before dark and they hurried and stumbled along, urged by fear, but found nothing more welcoming than the sheltered side of a tree bole out of the wind. The night seemed endless and cruelly cold and at first light they started off again, too numbed to have any clear idea of where to go. Suddenly Skyboy stopped to listen. Somewhere a great body was galumphing and snorting, thrashing around to pick up the trail, gnashing its teeth and stamping its hoofs.

'It's the Ollafub,' said Skyboy solemnly, 'and I think he has decided to turn BAD.'

They broke into a run and hurried as fast as they could through the frosty trees. The grass crackled underfoot and the hoar frost fell off the branches like white rain and their breath went up into the cold air like steam. They came to the edge of the forest and in front of them they saw the river winding away ahead, glistening white with the ice which nearly covered it.

'Come on!' shouted Skyboy. 'It's our last chance! We'll have to jump for it and hope the ice won't hold him!'

They raced on and could hear the Ollafub break into the open just behind them, his hoofs rattling on the stones. They reached the edge of the ice, their hearts pounding and their breath coming short—and then they stopped horror-struck because what had looked like a narrow ribbon of dark water from the bank was in reality yards and yards across and quite impossible to jump. The Ollafub was close behind and now quite sure of his victims. He leaped on to the ice with a triumphant bellow and stopped to execute a savage frisk and gambol. Stupid Ollafub! This was just what was needed. With a crack like a gun going off the ice on which the children and cubs were huddling broke free and started to float off down the black water, turning slowly round and round, displaying in the most tantalizing manner possible the Ollafub's escaping quarry. He was frantic with rage. He bellowed and he somersaulted and he bucked like a bronco and of course exactly the same thing happened to him. The ice on which he was making his contortions broke off with another crack and down the river went the Ollafub too, a little sobered at the sight of the icy water, but now more hopeful of catching up with his prey.

That was a nightmare journey on the ice rafts, now rushing over rapids, now coming almost to a standstill in the backwaters, sometimes widely separated, sometimes so close that only a few feet of water lay between them. Once the Ollafub tried to leap but his weight submerged the side of the icefloe on which he was standing and all he got was a ducking, cleaning up his 'hinderbits' to Tob's satisfaction. Once he leaped in the wrong direction and pulled himself

up just in time, because they were whirling so fast down a
rapid that the ice rafts had turned right round before he
could make his spring. For most of the time they were
going at a breakneck speed and must have travelled miles
before the river started to spread out into a wide lake, and
the water became shallow and nearly still, so that they
drifted around helplessly, sometimes far away from each
other, sometimes converging so terrifyingly close that all
hope seemed to be lost. But it was here that weight became
the deciding factor. The Ollafub's ice raft, which all the
time had lain lower in the water, grounded on a submerged
island and there he stuck fast, so that no bellowing, stamping or violent imprecations could move him. Hardly able
to believe in their fortune, Skyboy, Littleflame and the
three cubs floated away, watching the furious antics of
their enemy as he faded into the distance.

When they felt absolutely safe and the Ollafub was just
a speck on the horizon, Littleflame turned to Nob with a
mischievous grin.

'Do you think we ought to go back and rescue him,
Nob?' she asked.

Nob hid her face in her paws and did not answer.

It was not until the following day that they managed to
ground their ice raft on the opposite side of the river. They
were thankful to do so because the ice was beginning to
melt, they were standing in cold slush and wondering how
much longer it would carry their weight. They splashed
ashore very hungry and wet, but they had travelled so far
down the river that already the air seemed warmer and
there was a smell of spring. It was something to be rid
of the Ollafub and to be on dry land, however lost and far
from home they still might be.

Near where they landed a dusty road stretched away into
the distance from a ford across the river where wheelmarks

and footprints went down to the water's edge. As a road must lead somewhere, they started to follow it in the hopes of finding a village where they could beg food and ask the way. By midday their throats were dry from the dust and they drew off to rest for a while in a copse on the side of the road. They lay looking down over a small marshy valley and somewhere they could hear water running.

'Do you see what I see?' asked Skyboy, shading his eyes with his hand. 'Is that really a wheel turning all by itself in the middle of the marsh?'

'Let's go and look,' said Littleflame, and they crossed the marsh, jumping from tussock to tussock, and when they reached the wheel they found that it was being turned by the water gushing from a spring. Wooden cups were fitted to the wheel and as it turned it emptied its cups into a runnel which led away over the marsh. They followed the runnel until they came to a thick hedge. They pushed through the hedge and found themselves in a garden.

After the exposure of the river, the dust of the road and all the dangers that they had been through, this garden looked so safe and full of contentment. It was laid out simply with cultivated plots and walks lined with slender poplar trees, and every walk had its running stream, and fountains played in some of the plots and water fell from mossy basins into pools. But there was a strange thing about the garden. Here it was neither spring, summer, autumn nor winter but all four of them at the same time. There were apple trees covered with pink blossom and humming with bees, and underneath the blossom hung the apples all shiny and ready for picking. A newly-dug plot of earth was raked and friable for sowing, but out of the same piece of earth grew stately plants of corn, loaded with fat cobs splitting their jackets to show the pale gold seeds inside. Snowdrops and roses grew among the fountains and the roses had hips among the blossoms. Birds were singing in the poplars which waved grey and lacy against the sky, but on them were fresh spring buds and the tenuous yellow leaves of autumn shivering in the wind.

Skyboy heaved a great sigh and lay down and buried his face in the sweet-smelling moss. The bears settled down beside him, but Littleflame ran to and fro, peering into the plots and hurrying up and down the poplar walks. She had become very excited, and soon they lost sight of her altogether flitting away between the tree trunks.

You may have guessed what she was searching for, and she came to the end of her search quite suddenly where a green cedar hedge enclosed a small cobbled space and a fountain played in an old stone basin.

'Cottonshirt!' she cried, and threw herself down beside him. Her wish had come true. Ever since her strange adventure with the Snake Gypsies, when she had picked up the lost baby and had been thrown into prison, she had wanted to see Cottonshirt again. She had left him in such a hurry with so many questions unasked and now at last she had found him. She had known that this must be his garden, when she saw all the growing things embracing all the seasons together in a beautiful, magical, rhythmic disdain of every preconceived idea, and that nobody else but Cottonshirt could have tended these mysterious timeless trees and flowers.

Cottonshirt had been weeding the cobblestones, but now he sat down and she sat down beside him, and they watched the water gushing from the fountain and they talked. And it was quite a long time before the others grew tired of waiting and found them there, still sitting under the cedar hedge. Cottonshirt was pleased to see them all, and he took them to a little house which stood in the middle of the garden, and where he had a chair and a table and an inkstand and a pen, some books and some dried gourds with curly tendrils hanging from the ceiling. There he left them and went out through the window, which puzzled everybody except Littleflame, because he did not open the window, and it was glazed with small round bottle-glass panes. When they had finished tapping the glass and staring through it at the garden outside, they turned round to find five steaming bowls of soup on the table and five freshly roasted corn-cobs.

'It's meant for us,' said Littleflame. 'When we've had our supper we can go to sleep. He'll come back when he isn't busy.'

The first things that Tob had noticed when he came into Cottonshirt's house were the pen, the ink, and the books. When the others had gone to sleep he crept back and lifted one of the books from the shelf and placed it carefully on the table in front of him. He sat down and turned the pages one by one, examining each one from top to bottom. He looked just as though he was reading to himself, but of course he could not really read a word. He was so engrossed that he did not notice that a candle had lighted up beside him, and when he at last lifted his sleepy head to shake it and look around the room, to his surprise he found that Cottonshirt was sitting beside him. Tob blinked, feeling a little embarrassed.

''Tis times as I done wish as I kin read,' he said in explanation.

'It won't be very difficult,' said Cottonshirt, 'if you let me teach you.'

'Thee's kind,' answered Tob humbly. 'I'se nowt but a stoopid bear. 'Tis Tob as kin write, but 'tis Tob as can't never read.'

'Show me what you can write,' said Cottonshirt and handed him the pen. This was almost more difficult to manage than a potato peeler, but slowly and laboriously

Tob traced out the two words which had been written for him by the little house after his adventure with the goblins.

### TUP YATS

He had kept the paper for a long time and had memorized the letters and had never forgotten them since.

"'Tisn't never in that there book,' he said. "'Tis like she be tellin' I to bide still, but 'tisn't never them words.'

Cottonshirt took the paper from Tob and held it up against the candle with the writing on the other side. The light shone through and this is what he now saw:

### STAY PUT

Tob looked at it for a long time, then "'Tis widdershins,' he said.

'The first way is widdershins,' said Cottonshirt, 'and the second way is right. Come and I will show you in the book.'

They thumbed through the pages of the book together until they found the word 'STAY' and then the word 'PUT.' Tob was satisfied.

'I wouldn't never have knowed it by my own,' he said, wondering if, with the help of this magical personage, he would be able to realize his wish at last. To be the very first bear to learn to read—his head swam with the thought.

'We'll have a lesson every night and you'll soon learn,' said Cottonshirt, as though Tob had put his thoughts into words.

The lessons were kept secret so that Tob would be able to surprise the others. Little by little he mastered the letters and the sounds that each letter represented. Soon he could write and read short words. 'Boy', 'Girl' and 'Dog', and then 'Tob', 'Nob' and 'Hob'. The evening that he accomplished these he turned sadly to Cottonshirt and said:

'Our Cob done be deaded. 'Tisn't never no use writin' him.'

'Write him,' said Cottonshirt, 'and see.'

So he wrote 'Cob' too, and each of his seven words was on a separate piece of paper, and he rolled a little stick into the side of each so that he had made seven little flags and he stuck them up in the inkstand. And his heart was overflowing and he felt tremendously proud and he sat looking at them for a long time. And while he was looking at his little flags, somebody looked in at the window and that person had prick ears, a furry face and bright eyes. What he saw was a saintly old man at the table, a hunched-up small bear by his side, two more bears curled up on the floor, and a boy and a girl asleep on the benches. Tob looked up and saw the face at the window. He rubbed his eyes because he thought he was seeing something that was only inside his own head.

''Tis like as if our Cob done be come to fetch his'n,' he said to Cottonshirt.

'He has. Come in, Cob,' said Cottonshirt.

And Cob came in and a very live and kicking Cob it was, and with him came Thunder, all wags and licks and genuine delight. There was such a noise of hugging and kissing that Hob and Nob and Skyboy and Littleflame all woke up, and then there was more hugging and kissing, and Cottonshirt looked on just as happy and pleased as anybody.

Of course the five of them were longing to know what had happened to Cob, and Cob was longing to know what had happened to the five, so there was no more sleep for anybody. They sat and they talked and they talked until the candle burned itself out and the day looked in at the window. But as you already know what had happened to the five, there is only Cob's story left for you to hear.

When Cob fell out of the thorn tree, he had seen nothing but black jagged teeth of rocks rushing up at him from below. He did feel a tremendous bump, but it was not the kind of sickening end-of-all-things bump that he had expected, but a sort of squelchy plop. At first he could see nothing and could not imagine what had happened, then he found that he was struggling in a pool of mud. It was thick and dark and the consistency of porridge and nothing could have made a better landing ground for a fall. He floundered round until he found an edge, then he pulled himself out and tried to wipe his eyes. He looked up the cliff, hoping to see the others, but whether it was the mud in his eyes, the shock of his fall or the angle of the cliff, he found that he could see nothing. He tried to shout, but his mouth was full of mud and only a hoarse grunting sound would come. He wanted to cry, but he remembered that this was all part of learning to be brave, so he climbed higher among the rocks and tried to clean himself. But the mud was as sticky as could be and it was an impossible task, so he went off in search of some water. He found a river which he was sure had not been there before the earthquake. It was rimed with ice and looked terribly cold, so he decided to keep on his mud coat until the next morning.

And a very good thing it was that he did so. He sat miserably on the river bank, drying in the cold wind—and the mud hardened and caked, and he soon looked rather like an anthill that was rather like a clay model of a bear. Just as he was about as stiff and immovable as a pitcher, to his horror he saw a long string of Ollafubs approaching, loaded with cauldrons and huge long-handled spoons, and young Ollafubs sitting on the shoulders of the old ones.

The Ollafubs looked tired and disgruntled and dragged themselves along dispiritedly, and when they reached Cob they sat down in a ring, completely encircling him. He was terrified and if he could have run he would have, but his

mud casing kept him absolutely still, so he closed his eyes and tried to keep even stiller while he strained his ears and tried to hear what they were saying. It seemed that the earthquake had ruined the underground caverns where the Ollafubs lived. Some had been crushed by falling roofs, some had been drowned by underground torrents, some had been pinned down by rocks while trying to escape and were lying half-dead and helpless. (At this point in Cob's story Nob and Tob looked at each other very hard and nodded wisely.) None of the Ollafubs present had made any attempt to help the injured, but finding themselves free and unhurt had snatched up what possessions they could and set off in search of new quarters. They quarrelled and swore terribly while they talked, and slapped each other and slapped their children, and Cob wondered how they ever managed to live together without all getting murdered. They were arguing which way to go, and one group wanted to go one way and another group wanted to go another way, and after a great deal of shouting and cursing the largest Ollafub got up and stepped heavily into the centre of the ring and sat himself down, leaning his spiky, scaly back right against Cob.

'Hist! You bottle-eyed spawn of a decaying conger!' he began in a horrid guttural voice. 'Shut your gobs and listen. Over the river—fine village, beds, tables, caves above, all mod con—eat men, eat bears, move in— Haw! Haw!'

Cob prickled with horror. Caves! That was his home! Village! That was the children's home! He forced himself desperately to think of something he could do.

'What ab-a-a-t it?' asked the Ollafub, leering round the circle of his friends, then added endearingly, 'You stinking warts of a bilious wart-hog!'

Some of the Ollafubs started shouting, some started

singing, some just swore and bandied insults between themselves.

'To which! To who! Boggy old jackass!' shouted one.

'Lead us on, brother muckworm!' shouted another.

'Stow it, you mouldy bummer!' bellowed a voice from the back.

The big Ollafub's ear was very close to Cob's nose.

'Hark'ee!' said Cob in an awful sepulchral whisper. 'Hark'ee! Don't 'ee never go crossin' that there water an' don't 'ee never go near that there terrible place! 'Tis full up wi' girt dragons what's got out in the quakings. Hunderds an' hunderds an' hunderds of 'em!'

The big Ollafub scratched his ear and looked round. He could see nothing.

'Them there dragons is a-jumpin' an' a-bellowin' mad,' continued Cob. 'They chews an' bites up terrible small.'

The big Ollafub got up and stared all round and then sat down again. He was very puzzled.

'Tell me more, you midgetty, malarious mosquito you!' he hissed right down inside his back teeth so that the others could not hear.

''Tis I as tells 'ee then!' mocked Cob. 'Do'ee get on! Do'ee stick your girt hoofs in that there water an' there's girt, darn little fishes what's got pins for their toofies, an' what'll gobble you up so far as your girt elbows an' your girt nubbly knees, you girt, lumping effulump you!'

The crowd was getting very impatient. The big Ollafub had set himself up as leader, and all he was doing was to stare about and scratch himself.

'An',' continued Cob, driving home his advantage. 'Seein' as how you never done ask to come to this here place, what do be *my* place, an' you done sit yourselves an' sprawl yourselves like a mort o' nasty ole toads, if you isn't out an' away quicker nor winkie, 'tis I what'll call them dragons an' them little darn fishies what'll mince you up *an'* chew you up good *an'* proper!'

The big Ollafub was looking really uncomfortable. He was rolling his eyes this way and that, and peering first over one shoulder and then over the other.

'What are we stopping for, Brother Porky?' mocked a voice from the crowd.

'Who's Ole Man Moke na-o-ow?' This last sally brought a roar of laughter, and a voice struck up:

'Come on now! Ole Man Moke . . .!'

This was evidently the latest popular song among the Ollafubs (Nob and Tob again looked at each other), and the whole crowd of them, including the children in shriller voices, set up a roar, bellowing the song in a deafening chorus:

'Ole Man Moke wiv his bag of nuts
Bury him deep down under the mud!
The fishies is gobblin' his reverend's guts
The dragons is bottlin' his bones in blood!
To ho! To ho! To woddle oddle O!
He sets up his house on the side of the hill
He steps in the pani to swim to the shore,
His hoofs an' his hide may be floatin' there still,
But his little ole self isn't wiv them no more!
To ho! To ho! To woddle oddle O!'

This song, which must have sounded so prophetic on top of Cob's whispered warnings, was too much for the big Ollafub. With a bellow of fear he charged the circle, knocking the other Ollafubs right and left. They did not know what had happened, they were thrown into a confused panic, they seized their cauldrons and spoons and children and made off after him as fast as they could. Soon there was not an Ollafub in the place, only a confused pounding in the distance to tell where the rabble had gone. And not even

Cob could guess whether they had gone because he had made up that absurd story about dragons and fishes for the big Ollafub or whether they were really frightened by their own song. Perhaps it was a bit of both.

As soon as morning came Cob cracked the mud off himself, and without a moment's hesitation plunged into the icy river and swam across. He was as clean as a whistle when he reached the other side, and his spirits were soaring. He felt he could push over the world with one paw and made off as fast as he could towards his home. To his delight and relief he found the cave untouched by the earthquake, and Father and Mother Bear unharmed. He quickly told them all that had happened, then hurried on to the village. Thunder was waiting anxiously on the road as though he was expecting him. They waylaid a boy who was out searching for some lost goats and gave him a message to take back to the village, then without wasting any more time they set off together to find the others. And although at that time Skyboy and Littleflame and the other cubs were still on the top of the precipice, Thunder, who led the way, did not go in that direction at all, but started off down the bank of the new river on that long walk which led them in the end to Cottonshirt's garden.

The stories were told, talk was at an end, and they sat for a while pondering the strange results of a few wishes. Thunder lay across the doorway. Having gathered his charges safely together, he was going to keep them there. That was always his wish. But there were still two wishes unaccounted for—Skyboy's and Tob's.

'What did you wish, Tob?' asked Littleflame.

Tob leaned over the table feeling shy but important as well, and picked the seven little flags out of the inkstand.

''Tis what I done wish,' he said and handed each of them a flag and put Thunder's between his paws. ''Tis Tob as done write these here and 'tis Tob as kin read them.' They studied their flags with awe and felt tremendously impressed.

'What'll our Mam say!' exclaimed Nob, very proud of having so distinguished a brother. ''Tis Tob done be the firstest ever!'

''Tis Cottonshirt as done learn I,' said Tob, modestly anxious not to take all the praise.

Cottonshirt smiled and patted Tob, whose heart was too full to say any more.

'Now there's only Skyboy left,' said Littleflame.

Skyboy was fiddling with his coat and rubbing his fingers through his hair, making it stand on end like an unruly briar bush.

'You don't have to say,' said Littleflame, sensing his reluctance.

'It isn't that I don't want to say; I just don't know how to say it,' he answered slowly. 'I wished so hard and my wish was so huge that in the end I couldn't recognize it. I wished for something un-understandable and never-ending and mysterious and strange and very beautiful—whatever can it have been?' He rubbed his head again and then was silent and stared down for a long time at the floor in front of him. When he looked up they were all asleep, all except Cottonshirt, who was sitting cross-legged on the air floating in front of him.

'That was a good wish,' said Cottonshirt.

'It seems such nonsense now,' said Skyboy awkwardly, 'but it seemed important when I was wishing.'

'The greater the wish, the greater the cost, the greater the gain, the greater the loss,' said Cottonshirt.

Skyboy considered this enigmatic statement and shook his head. 'I don't really think I understand,' he said sleepily. 'Please explain what you mean.' But Cottonshirt had gone, away through the little, round bottle panes of glass where the sun was beginning to shine in and leave small bright circles of light on the wall. He had gone out to tend his garden.